A BABY FOR CHRISTMAS

A CHRISTMAS ROMANCE

MICHELLE LOVE

HOT AND STEAMY ROMANCE

CONTENTS

Made in "The United States" by:

Michelle Love

© Copyright 2021

ISBN: 978-1-64808-720-2

BLURB

Amelie: I hired Daniel to have a baby.

I am the only female billionaire in Louisiana. I want for nothing but a child ... and the right man.
Finding a good man, however, is tough. So I'll settle for a baby.
At least then I'll have someone who loves me.
A discreet advertisement is the solution:
One million dollars for a healthy male to stay with me long enough to get me pregnant.
Then he walks away, giving up all paternity rights.
It's a sweet deal. Of course, I have a lot of suitors.
However, charming, smoking-hot Daniel Fontaine is the only one I want.

So, Daniel and his daughter Caroline move into my mansion outside of Baton Rouge.
I thought losing my virginity would hurt. Instead, he turns it into a night to commit to memory.
And he does the same every night after.
It's taking a long time for me to get pregnant ... but I don't mind.
Sex with Daniel is a perk by itself.

It's not easy to keep from falling for him.
But can I trust him to be anything more than my baby daddy?

∿

Daniel: Amelie LaBelle is the perfect target.

Rich, lonely, isolated, and desperate for a baby.

Not to mention she's a gorgeous virgin itching to be swept off her feet.
The million dollars I get for knocking her up is chump change compared to what I'm after.
A wealthy wife with her heart in my pocket sounds a lot better to me.
She says my daughter and I can stay until she has her baby.
So I'll make sure she takes a very long time—and a lot of sex—to get pregnant.
By the time I'm done with her, she won't be able to live without me.

Maybe I'm a bastard—but I'll do anything to help my little girl.
Only wealth like Amelie's will make Caroline walk again.
All I have to do is keep my head, and make sure Amelie never learns I'm playing her.
The only problem is ... she's growing on me fast—and on my daughter, too.

This sham relationship is getting real, fast.
And when Amelie discovers some of my secrets, I'll have to fight to redeem myself.

1

AMELIE

I'm sick of spending the holidays alone.

Growing up, I always spent Christmas with crowds of people. This same sprawling country manor echoed with the voices of dozens of French cousins from my father's family. Their parents turned their noses up at me—the Creole daughter of a poor American mom—but the children just saw another playmate.

When my father died in a drunken crash, the crowds disappeared and his family turned their back on us. Christmas withered down to my mother, me, and maybe a few friends. My mom, an orphan, had no one but me—at least then, we had no one around to hurt us with their duplicity or scorn.

Now I'm in the same position: the only family I will get are children of my own. I'm thirty and unmarried. It's leaving me contemplating some pretty unusual options to fill up my lonely, vacant home.

Am I really going to do this?

This year, again, I'm having Christmas dinner alone, just like the last five, since Mother's death from cancer. I'm her only surviving child and the duty to continue the family line falls on me. But times like now, as I watch the growing storm wind stir the myrtle fronds outside, I wonder what to do to have a child of my own. And on my own terms.

The maids and other staff have gone home, aside from the security guards patrolling my mansion and grounds. The cook, Marcie, left a small feast of my favorites on covered plates: salmon with lemon and garlic, rice pilaf, tomato salad, a sliced Philippine mango, and a single glass of chilled Chardonnay. Cherry pie for dessert. Its crown of vanilla ice cream was melting so fast in the hot evening, I had to eat it first.

It's not very Christmassy—but neither is the weather outside Baton Rouge today. My Christmas lights adorn palmettos and trees in full bloom and fruit. No severed evergreens or fake snow to be found anywhere.

But, like everywhere else, the Christmas feast is about family. So here one is being planned.

I dine at a small bleached wood table on the screened balcony which peeks through the myrtles at the rolling lawn spreading out in every direction from my estate. This was my father's mansion; my father's money, though, in my hands, it has multiplied exponentially.

I get the occasional phone calls from France—now that I profit more annually than their country's GDP. I recall my mother, and our last lonely Christmases, and never answer. My cousins might have grown up into decent people but they're a package with their parents —whom I want nothing to do with.

That's why I dream of my own family, with my own children and grandchildren filling up this place. I used to dream of a husband as well—but time and disappointment have changed my ambitions. Since my mother died, I haven't even been on a date.

Romance is a gamble—one that has not paid off for me. But a baby?

It's so much better to care for a child on my own than spend another ten years playing the field, looking for a man to love me and start a family. I want to be a mother. A man's permanent participation in the process isn't exactly necessary.

And as much as I cried over Dad, genetic material and money were all he could supply. And I don't need money.

Looking down at my notepad, I've been making a list of considerations, sometimes crossed off. Sometimes they make me blush.

Intelligent

Fit

Healthy family history

Mentally stable

Responsible

No addictions

No family history of addiction

34-42

Dark hair (?)

Scratch out the dark hair. I don't actually care what color my baby's hair is. The sperm donor can be any race or color—as long as he's healthy, meets the other standards, and is willing to abide by my terms.

Apparently that was too much to expect of Louisiana men when I looked for dating and marriage prospects. Even if all I wanted was to keep the money I earned before the marriage. That's how to distinguish a gold-digger: if anything gets between them and my money, even if it's my own property, they get mad.

The rumble of thunder distracts me; the lowering sky tosses through the branches and I nod. *Not long now.* Staring at my list, I take another bite of my pie, barely tasting it.

A lot of financial, sexual, and romantic predators have been fended off. The last one was Marcus, who told me he would "lay down the law" as soon as we married, and that my estate needed "a real man" to manage it. By then, similar and worse encounters had burned me out, so I outright told him to go to hell.

I dab at my lips with a napkin; the delicate, girlie way. *I'm a bit of a bitch. But a lady in my position should be.*

I haven't given up on romance so much as on letting men and luck decide when I become a mother, and how long to spend alone. That gives strangers too much control over my life—and many of those strangers have turned out manipulative and hostile.

Rain starts falling in sheets, the smell of ozone promising a real summer thunderstorm. The wind lifts my curly brown hair away from my face as it sighs its way through the insect screens. It'll be a beautiful night.

The *Lord of the Rings* series is on when the thunder first rattles all the gem and mineral samples lining my living room walls in their cases. It's actually a parlor off my bedroom, but I don't spend much time in the vast spaces on the lowest level—not enough parties to justify it most of the time.

The thunder rolls again ... I scoop up the notepad and pick up the pen, taking a gander at my advertisement.

Are you a healthy single or polyamorous man between the ages of 34 and 42? Single woman seeks sperm donor for live-in arrangement. Discretion and a background check are required; must be willing to move in and relinquish custody rights.

Room, board, medical tests, and travel will be covered until conception is confirmed. Incidental expenses are negotiable. A substantial bonus is available for a successful full-term pregnancy.

Sitting back, I let out all my breath and nibble on the pie again, examining what is there so far. It seems cold, given the subject matter. Maybe it should be? Would it be too soft?

This is business. Even if it involves fucking me at least once a night until a pregnancy is established.

If my dating experiences do not improve, this might be the last time I let a man have sex with me. As well as the first. *Maybe I should be pickier.*

Dark hair goes back in. The sort of men who have always caught my eye are: Richard Armitage, Idris Elba, Hugh Jackman, and Mark Dacasos. The more personal parts of my list will not be printed; they are reminders for when the photos start coming in. Thinking about it, I add **hot** as well.

"Now you're just being shallow," I chuckle. But ... this situation will be awkward enough, no matter how hot a specimen plays my stud. *It will be even worse if I'm not attracted to him.*

A flash of lightning edges everything in a brilliant light for a moment and I brace myself for a brown-out, but the power doesn't even flicker. The plantation has been in our family for five generations; in my youth, the lights would flicker with every storm. Clearly, upgrading the power system has paid off.

Why don't you get out and meet more people, Amelie? It's the commonest thing my friends tell me. They don't understand that, after everything, I want tenderness, kindness. If a man cannot provide it, I would rather go without one.

My child will get my love and efforts instead.

After a few more hours of watching movies and fiddling with my ad copy, I retire to my bed. Lying alone on a mattress that could sleep four, I listen to the storm beating against the armored windows. My doubts gnaw at me for a while before drifting off.

What if no suitable man responds? What if someone else shows up who tries to use me? What if he's difficult to live with, or lousy in bed?

Maybe I should have done the artificial insemination after all. My eyelids start getting heavy. I'll feel better knowing my child's father.

And ... the idea of spending my entire life a virgin ... hurts.

Especially since it's hardly my fault. It's not like the bar was set particularly high for potential lovers. In this day and age, it seems that men will sometimes dig to get under the lowest bar.

Even my father did that.

My own bitterness is noticed with some amusement as I drift off. *It will probably be fine. Not every man is dreadful, and most of the respondents will be perfectly normal.*

One of them should be able to help me conceive in the course of a year. Provided, of course, someone is interested. There's always the lab, if not.

And so I advertised, anonymously, online.

2

AMELIE

Holy crap. Why in the world have I done this?

In just two weeks, I have received about six thousand applicants! Six thousand men who love the idea of getting paid to impregnate me, even sight unseen, with no name or mention of my wealth.

And most of them are very blunt about it.

Not only is romance dead, I think, but a lot of these guys can't even manage tact.

I sit in my book-lined office, overlooking the rear garden, scrolling through the archive of messages on my tablet. I disqualify anyone immediately who is from overseas, gives a hint of being married, or asks my net worth. That only pares things down by several hundred, however.

All right, this is ridiculous. There's no way I'm going to read all these emails from top to bottom. It's time to put on my executive hat and cut everyone who doesn't qualify.

First are those who refuse to follow instructions. It's as simple as running a computer program: there's no emotion involved in sticking to my list. I didn't make my first billion by being kind to those who didn't respect me.

I sort out the too old, too young, and those from outside a hundred-mile radius, cutting the list down to just about four thousand. I use the same cold detachment and adherence to facts that I use when hiring or firing at work. All the same, I feel flutters of fear as I send rejection after rejection and the consequential blocking of the applicants.

Thank you for your interest. Unfortunately, you cannot be considered for this position because you are ...

... Not from Louisiana.

... Still in your teens.

... Old enough to be my father.

All right, that went swiftly. I take a good swallow of my sweet tea before deciding on the next eliminating factors ... One way or another, get down to a short list of a few, maybe even just two men.

Thankfully I did not disclose my home address. The image of strange men trampling my lawn and flowerbeds, tracking dirt onto my pristine walkways and stately porch, makes me shudder.

How many would be angry if refused in person? How many would explode into online abusers if I gave them a chance?

Maybe it's silly to let strangers threaten me—even in big, angry crowds.

What exactly am I afraid of? I have money, power, and a small army's worth of security between me and any scorned suitor. Perhaps it's just instinctive, this urge to protect myself from the men who would use me without care.

I cut another nine-hundred odd applicants who are clearly trolling. A few at least give me a laugh. But none get a reply.

And after that ... the selection process becomes unsettling.

Two out of three left are so overtly and creepily sexual in their approach, they make me shudder with revulsion. There's over-excitement and awkwardness ... and then there's vileness, suggesting they either don't care about my comfort level, or maybe just want to see how much garbage I'll put up with.

I cut them easily, and send my formal rejections with a gleeful disdain.

Although you technically qualify for the position, you lack the social grace, consideration for others, and respect for women needed to make living with you for up to several months bearable. This decision was made based on your ...

... Explicit description of your sexual intentions, fantasies, and demands.

... Unsolicited and unwanted description or image of your genitals.

... Assumption of my interest in a submissive relationship.

... Repeatedly calling me "Mommy."

It seems that two-hundred odd of the remaining applicants want to preach at me for my "immoral" choice. The rejection pile grows ... I've been judged by every member of my family, with the exception of my mother, and see no point in putting up with it from an applicant.

That leaves eight hundred and ninety-six men. Staring at page after page of email messages, scrolling back and forth, figuring out other disqualifying characteristics. There's too many to interview. I couldn't even correspond with them all!

Frustrated, I scroll the included image files. Nudes, fetish wear, or bad imitations of Christian Grey get binned as well. The same goes for below-the-waist pics showing off bulges, real ... or enhanced.

Nice zucchini-smuggling job there, friend. I could have lived my whole life without seeing that. You are a walking argument for thoroughly rinsing one's produce.

I struggle on, bolstered by the brief laugh. But I'm getting tired, and even more frustrated. My rejection letters get increasingly vague, formal, and short.

I regret to inform you that the position has been filled. Thank you again for your interest. Send, block, and move on.

Five hundred and ninety-one left. My glass is empty and I stand up to stretch and get another refill. Outside, I can smell rain again, but right now the steam heat parches me.

My head throbs. I gently massage my temples, eyes closed, and swallow more tea. I'm at my limit, temporarily out of ideas for how to further narrow down the list.

Ready to quit for the day, I scroll back and forth through the photos, hoping for one of the men to catch my eye. And then ... quite unexpectedly ... one does.

His face flashes past as I scroll. It registers in my head. I stop and frown for a moment. In an instant, and in the midst of hundreds of other images, a pale-and-dark blur catches my attention. I slowly scroll back.

A pair of almost silvery-gray eyes stares back at me from beneath dark brows, gleaming behind a roguish curtain of jet-black hair. His skin is pale, his features a strange mix of generous and sharp, with a pointed nose and wide, sensual mouth. A smile lingers on those lips that makes my toes curl.

Oh, WOW! Hello.

He sent five photos. Tall and muscular, he looks as good in a suit and tie at a club as he does in shorts at the beach. I stare at the drops of water gleaming like pearls across his broad chest and feel my mouth go dry.

When I reach his last photo—I hesitate. In all these applications, I've seen just about everything—from genitalia to bizarre instructions from total strangers. But this one thing is unexpected.

He's smiling softly as he bends down to put his arms around a small, dark-haired girl in a wheelchair who's so obviously his daughter that a lump forms in my throat.

A single dad. It would be a package deal for the duration. And she's special needs.

I have the ability to accommodate her easily, so that's no reason to exclude him. *Besides, how can I say "no kids" when it's kids I want?*

So, instead of deleting his email, I open it up.

Hi, my name's Daniel Fontaine. I hope you're doing well. I'm a single dad in my thirties. I live in New Orleans where I own a small online investment firm and devote most of my free time to my daughter's care. I fit all your criteria, and you didn't mention having a problem with kids, so I thought I would give this a shot.

He follows it up with a current medical report, STD test results, and a genetic profile—a very nice addition, though more information than I actually need. I read over the rest, my gaze jumping sometimes to the thumbnails of his photos. Their effect on me is startling.

My cheeks get warm when I look at him! Shyly, I glance away and feel girlishly silly in doing so, as if the photograph is looking back at me. It's such an unexpected feeling, it scares me a little ... but a warmth stirs in my heart when looking at him smiling at his daughter easily counters that. It's not love at first sight ... but I wonder what he'll be like in person, if just an image leaves me this weak in the knees.

Is he as kind as he seems in that photograph? Maybe he won't mind my ... awkwardness. And wary. What concerns me right now is the awkward part, and the inexperience. Especially when it comes to sex.

I guess having an older child around would be good practice. Besides, I can hardly ask a man to leave his daughter home. I keep reading, deciding not to cut him out.

I have included the results of my recent physical as well. If more information about my health is needed, I can supply it. I'm a practicing martial artist; I don't smoke, and do not drink more than a beer or two a day.

My family's Cajun and French, and lives mostly on this continent. No health issues. A few smokers and one uncle who likes getting drunk, but nothing serious. The sole cancer death in my family was mesothelioma from asbestos exposure.

My daughter Caroline was disabled in an automobile accident three years ago. She is nine and undergoing physical therapy and surgeries in hopes she can walk again. Until then, she is confined to a wheelchair. I'm hoping this won't inconvenience you.

It would, but that still isn't enough to delete his email. Instead, I bookmark it and move on. I decide to at least look through the remaining hundreds of emails even as I know that Daniel has already set a high bar for the rest of them.

By the time I turn in, I've narrowed the applicants down to a dozen of the hottest, most eligible men in southern Louisiana, but it's Daniel's smiling face I see when I close my eyes.

3

DANIEL

I start checking my emails every few hours, eagerly waiting to hear from a wealthy single woman from Baton Rouge, looking for a man to knock her up. My application was sent three weeks ago, and I was warned the response might take up to a month, but Caroline's legs have been aching so bad that I'm getting desperate.

It took the dedicated work of two hackers, a private detective, and my own powers of persuasion to track down the mystery woman. Her fertility specialist gave up her name and details after a fat enough bribe. It hurt giving up the money, but if I play it right, I'll get it back a thousand-fold.

Amelie LaBelle, Louisiana's only female billionaire. A world-famous brilliant jewelry designer whose mining and production companies hold an enormous market share, and who single-handedly erased the debts of over a quarter of a million locals last Christmas alone. Smart, talented, rich, powerful, and soft-hearted—not to mention one of the hottest women I have ever seen.

Talk about my dream girl. Or at least, the closest I have seen since losing my wife.

"That's her!" Jerry grins as he returns with two longnecks from the kitchen. He's fair and chubby, with a perpetually boyish look, and is a house husband and new dad when not writing code—or tracking down people on my request. "And she totally wants your sperm, dude."

I drink in the gorgeous Creole woman on the screen; her elegant gown and tumbled dark-brown curls give her the look of a Greek goddess. Her eyes are a soft golden brown, like good bourbon. Her round cheeks and full, kissable lips, set in a shy smile, turn me on.

Robust curves, a cute face, and a demure manner. *What an intriguing combination.* "Damn, I hope so. Her idea of a 'substantial bonus' could pay for the rest of my baby's treatments."

"So how much for all of it?" Jerry frowns as he settles back in his chair. His own twins are tiny, and currently napping. The baby monitor sits next to his computer screen, showing their tiny, curled forms.

"The remaining surgeries are $1.2 million, including physical therapy. Designing a brain-controlled assistive walking exoskeleton to retrain her brain and muscles means more time and cash—up to another quarter million." My voice goes grim.

He takes a big sip of his beer. "That's a chunk of change, even with the kind of scores you manage. You don't think the bonus for knocking this lady up will actually pay for all of it?"

"No. But I'm hoping to persuade her to pay for it anyway." I'm very good at persuading people; in fact, it's my real business.

He lets out a low whistle and turns back to the golden-eyed goddess on the screen. "So what's your plan?"

"Buy us time," I reply cryptically. After over a decade in my line of work, I know better than to let anyone in on all my plans. "Buy myself time to convince her. It shouldn't take more than a few months."

His eyebrows rise as he takes another drink. "But your part will be over as soon as she's knocked up. How will you delay that? Stealth *on* a condom?"

I smile. "That's taken care of. I'll have at least until Christmas before having to worry about it."

Christmas. Roughly eleven months away. Long enough to make

sure my little girl got her legs back before the lovely Ms. LaBelle gets her baby. "Anyway, everyone will walk away happy."

If, of course, we walk away at all. Because that's my real ambition. Not only that my little girl walks again—I want to give her the life of a billionaire, to make up for my mistake.

"I really want to see you pull this one off, dude," Jerry chuckles over the chorused hum of his computer equipment. "How do you figure she'll choose you over everyone else?"

"Because, my net-surfing friend, I'm exactly what she's looking for." *If not, I'll find out what she secretly wants, and will become that man.*

"I hope she figures that out. Best of luck on this one, Danny boy. She's ... gonna be a tough nut to crack." He's looking at something on the screen besides her photo.

I curse myself for getting hung up on her picture without reading to the end. "No family on this continent, not much of a social life ... you couldn't find a thing on her romantic life?"

He shakes his head. "Bits and pieces, but nothing lasted more than a month. No signs of acrimony, she just ... stopped calling them and blocked them online."

Reading over the details he has gathered on her, they are added to the database on Amelie LaBelle building in my head from my various sources. "She's not happy with confrontation, especially with men."

"Probably not, Sherlock, but she didn't found and run so many companies because she's a wuss—or dumb." He scrolls to show me the rest. "She does have relatives overseas but they're not in contact."

Isolated, non-confrontational, probably lonely as hell—but with a strong will and mind, a lot of money to burn, and one simple desire. "No clue why she never married?"

He shrugs one rounded shoulder and burps. "Not entirely, but if her romantic life's been unlucky and her standards are high, well ..."

"Better alone than miserable with someone," I muse.

"Exactly." He tilts his head. "So ... saying you get the job, how do you plan on keeping from impregnating her if you're rawing her nightly?"

I stare at him and reprimand him with a sharp, "Jerry!"

"Okay, okay, none of my business. Just curious." He looks at me nervously.

I sigh, relaxing. "It's fine. Leave that to me."

Soon after that, the twins start crying. I help with a diaper change and give the poor guy some advice on properly giving a bottle. The two are cute, but from their thin blond hair and round faces, they, unfortunately, have inherited their dad's looks.

Hopefully, they'll also get his brains—but not his lack of social graces.

I walk out into the steamy rain with a thumb drive of files on Amelie in my pocket and her soft smile in my head. There's still a chance my initial hook won't be as good as somebody else's, and she won't even respond, but it's definitely worth a shot.

New Orleans in January is still a steam bath on days like today. The sky is low and a deep, saturated gray-black, with shadows of purple-like massive bruises. Right now, all we have is soaking rain and the occasional whip of wind ... but the feel of a real storm gathering behind it.

Get home to my little girl.

The wheels of my retired police car skid in the growing wind as the pavement becomes slippery from sheets of rain. I'm glad Caroline's not here. The skids and the way the wind rocks the big sedan would terrify her.

If anything, she's an even more nervous passenger; it's the trauma. I'm not sure what to do besides the obvious: soothe the nightmares, look after her when her upper back hurts, and do all I can to pay for every doctor's appointment. The bad memories and the growing levels of fear ... those I don't know how to fix.

Pulling into the lot at the extended-stay place in Metairie, the rain is starting to turn into spatters of hail and the sky is even darker. I get the cover onto the car and rush inside, hoping Caroline is holding it together until I am at her side.

When I enter our forest-colored, blandly decorated suite, Caroline is curled up on her bed near the big windows, quietly watching the storm. Her thin, pale little legs are limply stretched out in front of her and she's typing on her laptop propped on a pillow beside her.

She looks at me as I cross over to our small kitchen, her warm brown eyes so much like her mother's, it hurts to look into them. "Hey, Dad," she says in a tired voice.

"Hey, sweetheart. Up for some lunch?" She isn't doing well today; shadows around her eyes, and she's paler than usual.

She shakes her head, giving me a wan, apologetic smile. "Sorry, Dad. The pain pills are really tearing up my stomach."

"I'm sorry, baby. Do you think you can get a nutrition drink down at least?" It's our usual compromise when she can't eat.

She licks her lips and nods. "Okay, Dad. Strawberry."

I sit by her as she labors away, sip by determined sip. "When are we moving out of this place?" she asks as some of color returns in her cheeks. "I'm almost healed from the last surgery—we don't have to stay, do we?"

I gently smile at her She hates the residential hotel. It reminds her too much of our early days, when we were crammed into real hotels because there was little money and no honest work.

I gave up "honest work" for her. She doesn't know where the money comes from. But she's right—we need a real home.

"I have a job lined up near Baton Rouge. It should pay well enough for the rest of your treatment." I don't want to get her hopes up too high, since it's not yet confirmed. She needs some hope so much right now.

Maybe I do too.

"My back hurts today, Dad. Even with the pills." She presses her lips together and looks at me pleadingly.

I gently pat her on the shoulder. "It's the pressure changes from the storm. You're still recovering from where they fixed those three vertebrae, so they'll be sensitive for a while. It'll get better. Soon you won't need so many pills."

She sniffs. "Will the pain ever go away?"

I close my eyes, wincing, and hug her. "We'll do everything in our power to make sure it does, honey."

Even if that means seducing a billionaire for her money.

4

AMELIE

"So, Daniel Fontaine," my lawyer, Gloria Chan, taps her narrow, pursed lips with her fountain pen and peers at her laptop monitor. "Does in fact own a small investment firm in New Orleans. No local properties—he's currently living in an extended-stay hotel in Metairie with his daughter, probably to be close to her physical therapist."

I lean forward in the padded leather seat next to hers to peer at the screen. "No criminal record?"

"Not so much as a parking ticket. This guy's clean. And with the contract we just hashed out, he won't get away with much if you choose him. Legally, anyway." She smiles as she sits back for me to read.

"How was his daughter disabled?" I ask suddenly. Am I sniffing out the possibility of abuse? Maybe he seems too good to be true?

"Car accident. Here's the police report." She opens another tab. "Three years ago. His uncle Andrew was driving. He blew a .24 on a breathalyzer—three times the legal limit."

My throat suddenly tightens.

"His wife died at the scene, his daughter paralyzed and with a shattered spine, Daniel with two badly broken legs. Andrew walked away without a scratch." Her normally cheerful tone has gone grim.

"... Damn. Did he go to jail?" *Poor Daniel. And that poor, poor kid.*

"Yeah, died there sixteen months later after being shivved in a riot. Daniel was his last living relative and never picked up his ashes." She eyes me. "Can't actually say I blame him."

"Me neither," I breathe. "He's trying to fix what happened."

"His daughter was robbed of her mom and the use of her legs because her great-uncle lied about being sober." Gloria taps the pen between her fingers like ashes from a cigarette. "If that was my kid, I'd do anything to fix it."

"What about the interview?" I'm trying to keep calm.

"He was affable and polite. And startled when he learned who you were, the pay rate, and the bonus. Given the medical bills he is facing, that might be the reason he is so eager." Her chair creaks as she leans back.

Drawing a deep breath, I feel an odd flush of warmth. It's been a crazy and weary few weeks since I read Daniel's first email. Now, he's one of three finalists ... and the one I should not choose.

He affects me too much. I may not be in full control with him around.

Yet Shawn or Aaron both seem like safe bets ... but also boring by comparison. Shawn, a stable and predictable New Orleans architect, and Creole like me, who would have gained my mother's approval in a heartbeat. And Aaron, a medical illustrator from Baton Rouge, already with two kids in his open marriage.

They're both perfect. Neither one rings a single alarm. But neither one haunts my dreams like Daniel.

"Is something wrong, Amelie?" my lawyer asks with an owlish tilt of her head.

"No, it's fine." *I'll talk to him. See how it goes.*

"Set up the first coffee date with Mr. Fontaine," I say confidently. "Give him my private number if he wishes to call me ahead of time."

She presses her lips and looks at me silently for a few seconds, as if considering something, but finally just nods. "I'll try to nail it down tomorrow afternoon," she says, and types in a few notes.

Walking out into the misty afternoon, I hear a distant ambulance siren piercing the fog. Instantly, I think, not of Daniel himself, but of his daughter—that little girl with shattered legs and spine, a little girl my money might be able to save.

I should just offer whatever she needs. I've saved people before. Sometimes it's the only thing that keeps the loneliness at bay.

This world is dark and cold but I have gained the power to bring some light to it. I can't win the approval of my father's family, or bring back my mother, or find a man to love me. But if modern medicine can make that girl walk again, and only lack of money stands in the way ...

I could save a good-sized country's economy with my money. Who am I to refuse this one girl?

This could work well for all of us. I get my baby, his medical bills get paid, and his daughter gets her last surgery.

The street is crowded despite the dreary weather. It's warm; my cream gauze duster and tank dress cling to me in the breeze. Walking, I feel another warmth rise up inside me again.

He has a better reason than lust or greed to shack up with an unfamiliar woman and give her a baby. And I can't stop thinking about him. There's nothing wrong with the other two ... except ... they're not him.

They're not Daniel.

Someone does a test-tug at my tan leather purse strap and I turn at once—to see a retreating back and crop of dark hair. *Ugh, for a moment it escaped me how much I hate crowds.*

The good feelings distracted me—but not enough to fall prey to a pickpocket.

Maybe I should go out with a driver instead of incognito, I think, returning to my small silver hybrid and settle into the driver's seat. But sometimes I wish to go unknown, quietly visit shops, and go about my business.

Fortunately, the tug at my purse strap is the worst thing to deal with until the safety behind my gates. *Well, that's that. My first pick among the finalists is having coffee here with me tomorrow.* I stroll through my doorway.

I stop, my heart suddenly pounding. *Oh no! What to wear?*

Locking the door behind me, I hurry up the stairs into my dressing room, dashing past my startled butler. "Is everything all right?" small, sleek Edmund asks, his mild blue eyes narrowing in concern.

"Uh, stand by for a refreshment list for tomorrow's coffee, and possibly an emergency call to my seamstress."

My dressing room is organized meticulously by color and the jewelry set they were chosen to go with. Black with diamonds, opals and rubies, sea colors with sapphires and pearls, forest colors with emeralds, earth colors or white with turquoise and amber. The cloth is just a backdrop for the gems and their settings—my art, and the source of my fortune.

I've only worn about half of the outfits here. My mother took me shopping all the time while Father was out on "business trips" with his newest young secretary. We would come back hours later, laden with bags, and I would tuck them away and forget about them.

I take the brown jasper and coral set and hang it up along with my belt and purse, discarding the outfit into the hamper as I dive straight into a frenzy of trying things.

Part of me thinks, *this is ridiculous. He's the one who should be trying to impress and attract me. It's my money and my decision.*

The rest of me wonders what his favorite color is.

I finally settle on orchid purple and soft pink, a silk halter dress with an empire waist and a flowing skirt. It goes well with the set of pink jade flowers and purple tanzanite in rose gold.

Two weeks just to carve those flowers. The carved rosebud dangles into my ample cleavage. Will he have the taste to appreciate it?

What just happened worries me a little.

This isn't a date. This is a business arrangement. Stop being so nervous!

But I can't help it. And because the feeling is laced with an unfamiliar, giddy happiness ... do I really want to?

5

AMELIE

The night was spent tossing and turning, second-guessing every decision about the arrangement, my clothes, the coffee service, everything! All morning was ridiculous—too nervous to eat, fussing endlessly with my hair and makeup, spending too much time choosing a perfume. I wait for Daniel, giddy and silly, as if, instead of arranging a human stud service, it's my first date with a new lover.

You haven't even met him! I check myself in the entryway mirror. *You don't know what sort of man he is living under the same roof.*

He's clean of disease and Dr. Weiss confirmed he is healthy with a high sperm count. Keep calm today and keep alert. Learn about the man himself.

Returning to the armored foyer windows, I look out past the porch to the gate at the base of the small hill. He's not due after three times; annoyed, I walk away.

Oh, come on. Amelie, you have all the command in this state of affairs. You're literally renting him out. He's in a financially desperate situation you'll solve if he gets the job. You can have him tossed out in three seconds, if need be.

You don't have to impress him. Really.

No matter how forcefully I tell myself that, the moment the gate intercom crackles, I jump to the control, allowing his old black sedan to enter.

He drives up, parks, and comes to me in loping strides across the raked white gravel of the driveway. He's wearing a dark, well-tailored suit and a tie that matches his lovely pale eyes. He bounds up my porch steps with the eager energy of a more youthful man.

I close my eyes, steadying my breath, reminding myself once again, I am in control. He knocks. My eyes open and I move toward the door. I put on a small smile, ignore the urge to beam, ignore the equally strong urge to retreat into the depths of my home in a fit of shyness ... and open the door.

His face beams up sincerely and his gaze falls on me. "Ms. LaBelle," he bows slightly. "Am I late?" He has a plain but well-maintained leather briefcase at his side.

"Right on the nose, Mr. Fontaine. Please come in. My office is upstairs." I step back to let him in and watch his gaze flick around briefly to absorb the entrance before returning on me again.

"Thank you." His eyes twinkle as he passes me. My throat tightens as his scent hits me. Manly musk and hints of spicy cologne, easily detected in the heat, as he closely slips past. I close the door, trying to ignore its enticement.

He walks toward the staircase, moving slowly as he looks around. My breath catches at the sight of his tight ass and broad, muscular back. The cloth straining across his shoulders makes me wonder what his muscles would feel like, tensing under my fingertips.

I want this one. No one else will do.

"Welcome to my home." I sweep ahead of him, so the view won't make me stumble on my own staircase. "Please follow me."

"Of course." His steps are surprisingly light. We get to the second floor, where my office door stands open with the fans running and gauze curtains drifting in the breeze.

"It's lovely," he comments as we walk. "Is this a family property, or a purchase?"

"It has been in my family for over a century." *Even his voice is attractive.* Low and resonant with a music to it. Does he know its power, or is he using it on purpose?

He may be oblivious. His manner is pleasant, and a touch flirtatious, but opaque. Examining his micro-expressions would get me gazing at him. How does that make me feel?

Worse, he might notice. He cannot learn how much influence he already has over me. When his eyes twinkle at me, it feels like I'm about to float.

That's bad. It's nothing I can afford. Money? No problem. My heart? That I have to guard.

My poor mother was a miserable example. *You do right by our family. Make us a success. Those snotty bastards think we can't make good on our own now that your daddy's dead.*

I paid dearly to make sure you could have a future with all the money you could ever need. Now go make me proud.

She paid dearly. In tears, in humiliation, in my father's infidelities and lies. She stuck it out, never divorced him—to ensure my future.

And I went out, worked hard, succeeded, and made her proud. My child will do the same as I will, provided the love, a fortune, and a duty to those of us who came before.

The thoughts take some of my dizziness away; I focus back on my guest, leading him to the office door. "Before coffee, I'll conduct a private interview that will take about fifteen minutes. We'll start with questions you might have, and go from there."

How am I keeping my voice so even?

"As you wish," he says simply, and follows me inside.

I settle in at the desk, and he sits across, flinging one leg over his knee and folding his hands over it. He looks completely at home! I'm not sure what to say for a moment. Fortunately, he's content to fill the silence.

"Why are you having a child this way, instead of going to a laboratory? I understand it could have been handled discreetly and that you would have been able to pick the genetic traits of your donor." His voice is gentle but his curiosity makes freezes my smile.

Many reasons. So many tears shed over those reasons. "You're very direct." No annoyance or defensiveness; just stating a fact.

"It's best we are honest with each other," he replies in a quiet, earnest tone. "My daughter's life will be greatly affected, for good or bad. Let's be sure there are no miscommunications or knowledge gaps that might lead to problems."

"Of course!" My cheeks are getting warm. The practical part of my mind wonders if his daughter is an excuse to be nosy, but he has a point.

"Does she know why you would move here?"

"She knows I'll do some work for you, but not the nature of the work. She's only nine and may not understand her daddy putting himself out to stud."

He says this as smoothly and pleasantly as everything else, catching me completely by surprise. He looks at me, and the warm twinkle of humor disarms me completely. A moment later, he continues more seriously, "Now, about my question?"

I swallow and nod, nervously pushing out an answer. "A lot of women who hire a man to impregnate them want to know the father at least on a basic level. Not to force any more involvement, but rather—"

"Is that your reason? I'm not interested in a general answer." His voice sharpens just the tiniest bit and my throat tightens a little.

"Yes. A large part of it, anyway. A more traditional approach is not possible. Nor do I want to treat conception like ..." I hesitate.

How do I tell a stranger going to a clinic felt like giving up? I couldn't even make a call for an appointment! How barren and sad it felt when I contemplated it? I want a child by a man's touch, not by a test tube.

Would a strange man understand that?

"Like a mere medical procedure." I look awkwardly out the window, over his shoulder. A flock of small, dark birds obscures the view for a moment as it rises into the misty sky.

A sudden stab of melancholy comes over me, so deep that I can't look at him for a few moments. He need not know about my sad romantic life. He doesn't need an explanation of every how and why.

He's a stranger. A hot stranger, and one who has enough information to trust me ... but the deep loneliness behind my decision—that he will not learn. He may just take advantage, if he does.

"You look gloomy," he comments, and my attention goes back to him in embarrassment.

Shit. "I'm fine." I take a moment to focus and look up as calmly as possible. "Do you have any further questions?"

"Yes. What will my schedule look like?" His voice is gentle but with the confidence of a man who already has the job. I can't resent it. It does, however, make me worry my emotions are easy for him to read.

"Hours?" I cough into my fist, blinking rapidly, realizing I never considered the specifics of our ... conjugal visits. "Ten to two, nightly," I say finally. "The rest of the day is yours, except for a few medical visits."

He nods. "Dr. Weiss?"

"Yes. I'm assuming you'll need time for clients and your daughter's school commute and medical visits."

"Yes, and physical therapy. Is this place accessible?" His brows draw together; his tone and manner that of a concerned-dad. It's even more disarming.

"There's a personal elevator that was put in for my mother after her health declined. I'll arrange for Caroline to have the bedroom next to it." Now I'm doing it—talking as if this is a done deal.

He nods in satisfaction. "Ah, good. So, ten to two."

"Barring emergencies, yes." He looks more amused. My stomach flutters. Is he considering what to do to me first?

"Sometimes my daughter has a rough night, but barring that ..." He strokes his chin and then flashes a brief, naughty grin that makes my toes curl in my pumps. "Four hours, though. Nightly?"

I refuse to be knocked off balance by this amazing, intoxicating man. "Yes. Until we can confirm a pregnancy."

The twinkle in his eyes becomes a gleam. "I've always wanted to test my stamina."

It's the most overtly sexual thing he's said so far and is subtly scandalous enough to leave me blushing and aroused. "I have no idea how long it takes—" I say hastily, and immediately know it was a mistake.

His eyebrows rise. "A virgin?" He notices my expression and hastily adds, "Sorry. It's a surprise when a beautiful woman tells me that."

I dig my nails into the silky fabric covering my knees, glad my hands are hidden from his view. "Until now, my priorities have been education, family, and work. I'm also very selective."

"Then I should be honored," he replies in the same smooth tone, his lazy smile returning. "Why did you choose me, anyway?"

My mouth goes dry. Tell him he's the only one among them I think about at night. He's the only one I want to fuck. "There are actually three finalists."

"But you chose me first," he observes. I lick my lips instead of answering. His eyes narrow in amusement. "Do I have an advantage over the others?"

Trembling, my gaze sweeps over him. When our eyes meet, the searing heat of his interest makes me realize the other two finalists do not matter. I want Daniel.

And he knows it.

"Besides meeting all my criteria, the dedication to your daughter was particularly notable." The half-truth sounds weak: an excuse. "It's not as common among fathers."

His sly smile fades and he tilts his head in curiosity. "It depends on the dad. I know several who would walk through fire for their kids."

And every single one of them makes me jealous. But never mind that. "That is true. I simply don't have experience, so found it notable."

He watches me silently. In that moment it dawns upon me what I have admitted. Suddenly, I'm a little frightened. *I have no control around this man.*

"Well, that's it for my questions. Do you have any for me?" He tucks his hands behind his head, broad chest flexing under his sleek suit, eyelids lowering like a contented cat's.

"I'll let you know. Your advance is fifty thousand dollars, plus expenses. You'll receive it upon move-in, in cash if you prefer."

I hesitate ... then find myself offering more than intended. "If you need assistance with medical bills during that time, let me know and we can work something out."

His eyes light up. "I appreciate that."

I relax. *He's not manipulative. He's just a dad jumping at a chance for his daughter.* "Would you like to come down for coffee now?"

"Absolutely. Mind if I take it iced? I'm parched." He winks as he rises from his seat.

"Of course."

6

AMELIE

Iced coffee with muddled mint leaves, chocolate and cream swirled into them. The tall glasses sit between us as we take seats on my beloved balcony. In two silver bowls, thin slices of chocolate cake support fans of strawberry atop clouds of whipped cream. A pyramid of finger sandwiches, mostly smoked salmon with cream cheese and cucumber, sits on a plate by the desserts.

"I could get used to this," Daniel says, saluting me with his glass before taking a long sip. His eyes squint with pleasure; his muscular throat works, and my fingertips want to reach and feel his skin. "You live in this palace by yourself?"

"Our family used to be much larger," I reply quietly and he goes silent, focusing on his drink as I watch him.

"If it's the family home, it would feel weird selling it and living somewhere else." He grabs a sandwich and bites into it with a grunt of enjoyment.

"That's exactly it. That, and honestly, my father's family has gone back overseas, so it's up to me and my descendants to fill this place up."

The coffee gives me a rush of energy; I've barely eaten since this date—er, *appointment*.

"I'm starting to understand where you're coming from," he muses, seeming intrigued. Or is it just projection? I hope not.

"I do have a couple more questions, now that I've thought about it," he starts, setting down his glass. "Where is my room?"

"That depends on your preference," I say very carefully, aware of my heartbeat picking up. "There are six bedrooms on this level, besides mine and your daughter's." *And I'm still talking like he's got the job.*

Is he calling the shot, or are my hormones?

"You're probably used to sleeping alone." I do my best not to bristle.

"I'm a very light sleeper." Again, no point in getting into details.

When my father's lover wandered drunk into my bedroom, nude and strange, wobbling toward my bed in the dark, I started locking my bedroom door and sleeping lightly indeed. He took me shopping for a new bedroom set, bribing me with chocolates and cash not to tell Mom. But she already knew.

"Understandable. So, this place ... can we use its facilities while we live here? You have a pool. Swimming is good for my girl's rehab. Would that pose a problem?" He's a little tentative, and I am less worried by my own vulnerability.

"Absolutely not; so long as someone is supervising, she may use the pool whenever she likes." The sandwiches are on slivers of toasted sourdough, sprinkled with dill seeds; they crunch pleasantly between my teeth.

Maybe it's all right we're acting like it's a done deal. This is comfortable ... aside from my ridiculous shyness. He's thoughtful, he seems to like me, we get along all right ... and I want him in my bed.

Maybe the last part is the most important: the primal instinct that overrides intelligence and leaves me impatient to hold him. The part that wants a child of his blood—his out of six thousand men.

I nibble on the treats and watch him eat as we chat; he tells me about his daughter, her love of drawing, how much she wants to settle somewhere and have a dog. I tell him about the house, the few off-limits places—mostly the kitchen and my jewelry workshop, as well as my bedroom—and about my own schedule.

"So you've taken a partial hiatus from your company?" He leans forward and puts his chin in his hands. "Who runs the show in your absence?"

"I still have the final decision, but the board handles most day-to-day issues for the next two years." It might not be the most ambitious move but my mother would understand. My shareholders were less sympathetic but ... I'm still the majority stockholder and what I say goes.

"What are you hoping for?" That smile. *Stop it!* It's too sweet, too warm, and too sexy! I want to see it every day!

"Um ... raising a girl would probably be simpler since what she'll be going through will be familiar to me. But any child is a blessing." That's the most diplomatic response I can offer.

"Daughters can be a handful. I try to be a good dad, but I'll be out of my depth the moment she hits puberty." He laughs ruefully and I laugh with him.

It feels really good.

"You don't have a boyfriend who will get jealous, do you?" he asks in that same mild tone. One tapered fingertip nips up a bit of cream from his dessert, and then disappears between his smirking lips. The sight of a brief, pink flick of his tongue catches my attention and I look away.

"No, I haven't been ... that is ..." *How does he do this to me?* I busy myself draining the last of my coffee from the melting ice cubes. *Calm down!*

"I don't date," I finally manage.

He tilts his head in a curious, almost animalistic way, his pale eyes staring unblinkingly into mine. "Why?"

I catch one of the ice cubes between my teeth and bite down on it. It grinds between my teeth and goes down my throat. I suddenly want to tell him it's none of his business. But instead, "It wasn't going well," is uttered.

For a split second, concern darkens his eyes—and he looks away again, mortified. I despise pity, like my mother.

He doesn't ask about my dreadful romantic life. Instead, in a gentle, warm tone that comes out smooth as honey, "You must have a case of skin famine."

I look back at him, eyes wide, and see him licking a bit more cream off his finger with a naughty gleam in his eye. "Skin ... famine?"

"Skin hunger. The need to be touched. Most of us have it at least to some degree."

"I suppose," I murmur, suddenly very uncertain again. Warmth and a weight fill me up, and his hand gently covers mine.

"Maybe I can be of some help there too." I start trembling again. His fingertips caress the back of my hand, sending jolts to the pit of my belly. "The way you look at me ... I'm *eager* to get started on that baby, if you are."

Oh God. "I ..."

"Don't tell me you're not curious." He stands. I get up as well and he moves closer, looming over me, his masculine scent clinging to my nostrils. "I don't imagine you'll want to spend months trying for a baby with someone who doesn't know how to fuck."

His sudden intensity catches me off guard; breathless, I stare into his eyes as he squeezes my hand and draws me so close, his shivery breath is on my cheek. His powerful body brushes against mine and his free hand slides up my arm in a light caress. "Sure you wouldn't like a taste?"

His voice is low, full of heat. I stare mutely back at him, astonished by his bold proposal ... and by how appealing it seems.

When it comes to doing anything sexual with a man, I've always taken it slow—glacially slow. My stomach contracts with a flood of shyness.

Tell him to go away. Make up an excuse. He's just a finalist; he hasn't won yet.

But he has. When I first looked at his photograph; when I thought of him every night; when he proved time and again that he's exactly what I'm looking for. Not just a sperm donor for the child I crave but a lover for the duration.

I wrestle with myself, close enough that his warmth settles against my skin like summer sunbeams. And then ... then he does the worst thing possible.

He reaches out for me and wraps me in his arms, his broad chest becoming my pillow. "Come here."

No, don't, I think, a moment before he cradles the back of my skull as the warmth inside my chest spreads through me. *Don't be so sweet.*

Too late. He holds me, tenderly enough that I could break his grip ... but I melt against him instead. He's warm and solid and his hand slides up and down my back in a stroke that leaves me weak in the knees.

"Oh," I murmur, feeling his burly back under my palms and his heartbeat against my breasts. It's been so long since anyone held me that my heart aches. And I can't remember a man being this tender.

A faint rattle of him pushing aside my plates before he returns to stroking my back. Every caress leaves me warmer and looser, the ache slowly burning away as the heat of his touch brings my focus to the present. Not in my sad past, but now, in my mansion, with a man who will do anything to me that I want.

I look up at him—and his kiss steals my breath.

His warm, firm lips touch mine, catching my lower lip between them, brushing against the corners of my mouth. I feel the dart of his tongue and whimper softly, parting my lips a little more.

His hands fondle my hair and back, slide over my shoulders, grip my hips and pull me closer. I can feel his erection, steely and substantial, brushing against me through his clothes. I close my eyes, feeling the craving so intensely that my thighs squeeze together.

Leaning back against the table as he bends over me, a low rumble of contentment vibrating his lips against mine. His tongue claims territory inside my mouth again, caressing and withdrawing, and I feel his hand slide smoothly over one of my breasts.

If I did not want him so badly, his audacity would earn him a slap.

But all I can do is moan, my leg sliding against his as I press closer to him.

Skin hunger indeed. He was right about that—right about many things. The more he caresses me, the closer he gets, the more I want. It's like the first taste of food after a two-day fast: glorious, intoxicating, whetting my appetite for more.

Then, gently, almost reluctantly, he lets me go. I stare at him, breathless, leaning on the table, aching from the loss of contact ... but also, on a certain level, relieved. He could have taken things a lot further, and I would have been swept into it, completely at the mercy of my desire.

It felt lovely. But I don't actually want to lose my virginity on the top of the balcony table. And he's too much the gentleman to take it there.

"So," he purrs as he helps me onto my feet. "Where do I sign, and when can we move in?"

I take a shivery breath. "My lawyer will send the release forms to your hotel tonight ..." I manage, sounding fragile—and completely enthralled.

He smiles, conquest gleaming in his eyes.

7

DANIEL

I want to crow, wheeling Caroline up the newly-installed wheelchair ramp and onto the porch of our new home. Her eyes are so wide! "Is this where we'll be staying?" she breathes in amazement.

"Yep, for at least six months. I'm hoping for longer. It depends on how much work Amelie's got for me." *And by work, I mean keeping her good and seduced. But you need not know that, honey.*

"So, Miss LaBelle's will let us stay through the rest of my surgeries too?" She sounds hopeful and less tired than in months. Hope is a heck of a drug.

Also not having to live on hotel food in a small suite with few services; nothing to do but watch TV and nowhere to go. "Yes, at least that. She wants to make sure you are comfortable here."

I almost feel a bit guilty. It's clear that under the stiff guardedness, Amelie is a very kindhearted woman. She doesn't deserve to be used.

On the other hand, she probably won't mind if I parlay a few extra months of good sex and good company into working legs for my daughter. She doesn't have to know our prolonged affair is intentional. Only how good I can be for her.

"I'll take your belongings upstairs." Amelie's butler—in all the excitement, I've already fucking forgotten his name—bows his neat, balding head and transfers our suitcases to a small luggage cart. I nod distractedly.

"Thank you!" Caroline says and he smiles politely, but his eyes twinkle.

Likes kids, huh? That's a good sign. Though, honestly, I can't imagine Amelie hiring anyone who doesn't.

I had it in the bag the moment our lips met. That little tremor that went through her, the way she stretched against me, the way her hands slid up my back. The disappointment in her eyes when I let go.

Keeping the surprise from Caroline for a day and a half was rough. But it's all paid off now. I've won, and she's delighted.

When Amelie appears at the top of the stairs, a fat folder and a pair of keys in her slender hand, my gaze slides over her hungrily. She's in a sea-green dress to complement the cluster of sapphires and emeralds at her throat; the silk clings to her, its layers fluttering around her like butterfly wings.

Tonight, I think—and then quickly push that out of my mind before it arouses me in front of my daughter.

"Welcome," Amelie says. Her gaze drops to my daughter and she smiles. "I'm Amelie LaBelle. Has your father told you about me?"

Not all that much. But, of course, Caroline has done her research anyway.

"You're the jewelry billionaire. You still make your designs. Is Dad doing your investments?" Caroline's tone is bright and probing.

Amelie blinks in surprise. "He is assisting me in one of my future ventures," she says carefully, and I relax. She's not the best liar, but she's trying to keep from confusing or upsetting my daughter.

"I'm really glad you're letting us stay here," she replies, changing the subject. She's already sensed there's more to this, but she's not the nosy type. Otherwise, I would have been in trouble years ago.

"I have more than enough room. And I've grown tired of living alone." Amelie smiles sadly for a moment before her expression brightens. "Well. Let's give you the tour and get you settled in your rooms."

She's all business again, despite her warmth toward Caroline. Her voice is smooth, her manner unruffled. She's in control again ... and it only tempts me more.

The gentle-hearted, desperately lonely virgin hiding inside this cool, competent heiress and businesswoman intrigues me. But her carefully cultivated act has an appeal. One would never know how quick she was to tremble and cling to me.

She's so smooth, sweeping through the halls and rooms of her plantation home like a princess. It makes me want to heat her up, to rumple her clothes and spread her curls across a pillow. As I help Caroline wheel her chair along the tour and into and out of the elevator, my cock starts getting hard in spite of my best efforts.

I imagine her sea-colored dress discarded on the floor of Amelie's luxuriant bedroom as she writhes under me. I imagine pleasuring her so well that she begs for more; so well she barely notices she's not getting pregnant for longer than expected. I got into this so my little girl can walk again ... but right now, the word keeps beating in my brain.

Tonight.

Maybe even sooner, if I play things right.

"And this will be your room, Caroline," Amelie says, far too long later. She opens the double doors leading to Caroline's suite—and shocks me.

The entire room has been redone in the same shades of blue as the outfit Caroline wore in the photo I forwarded. There's an adjustable bed with space on either side for her wheelchair, an accessible bathroom, a television, computer, and snack fridge. I stare at Amelie as Carline lets out a cry of delight and smiles mischievously, her nose wrinkling.

"Oh wow. This is amazing." Caroline rolls in, looking around with even wider eyes. She turns to Amelie as if half expecting it's a joke. "Are you sure?"

"Of course." Amelie's smile warms, more of her kindness coming out in her expression. "I will need your father at odd hours, and both you and he should be comfortable for the interval."

"Um ... thank you. I don't really know what to say." She sounds a little choked up.

Amelie notes this immediately and moves toward the door to give us some privacy. "I'll let the two of you settle in. Daniel, I'll be in my rooms when you're done."

A hard jolt runs the length of my cock at her simple statement, and I nod. She leaves, and I turn to my daughter, who is still processing all of this.

"Dad, is this really happening? I get all of this? And the surgeries, and no more hotels?"

"For as long as I can manage, yes. And by the time we leave, we should have enough to get us a small house somewhere." Or, if the lovely young heiress gets wrapped around my finger enough, we can stay forever.

As I help my daughter unpack into the low wardrobe, we talk about the rest of the day. She wants time to herself. Her back hurts and the pain pills are making her groggy again. Once she's in her sweatpants and T-shirt and settled on her new bed, I kiss her forehead and smile at her.

"You need anything before I check with the boss?"

"We'll have dinner later, right?"

"Yeah, probably the three of us. You'll love it. The food here is great."

"Good. I got tired of room service ..."

I make sure she's resting comfortably before stepping out. I cross the hall to my room next to the enormous master bedroom. It's luxuriant and masculine, dominated by a mammoth wood-frame bed. I toss my coat on top and make sure my bags are here. Then I eagerly walk out again.

My cock aches and throbs, uncomfortably constrained by my trousers as my anticipation grows with each step to Amelie's door. It's obvious what's in that folder, and those keys are mine. The papers are signed, the deal is sealed, and I'm about to be fifty thousand dollars richer.

But right now, all that is gravy. The real fortune is waiting on the other side of this door and every instinct tells me to go there and make her mine.

I'll spoil her. I'll make her feel so good that she'll have more trouble letting me go.

I gently knock on her door and put on my softest smile as Amelie opens it. "Caroline's napping." I step inside. She nods and closes the door behind me. She gasps as I brush against her and I turn so quickly that it's almost a reflex.

I take her in my arms—and the money, the keys, the long con, even Caroline—all slip out of my mind. There is only Amelie and her body pressed eagerly against mine.

8

AMELIE

I can't remember how we get across the room. Daniel carries me while he is kissing my breath away. By the time he starts taking off my clothes, I am too delirious with pleasure to let shyness stop me.

The afternoon breeze sighs over my half-bared body as I lie on my bed with Daniel crouched over me. I'm trembling, my nerves tingling wildly with desire and pleasure and my head full of a glorious warm fog.

My silk dress is on my bedroom floor. My shoes are by the door. My necklace and earrings hang from the bedpost like Mardi Gras beads.

My bra is somewhere in the tangled bedding. I don't care.

He tears off his shirt as he kisses me, mouth rough and hungry, his hands so impatient, a couple of buttons pop off and clatter on the floor. *That's all right. If he keeps making me feel this good, he'll get a hundred shirts.*

He throws the wadded fabric to the floor and strips off the T-shirt beneath; a wall of rippling muscle stretches over me as he pulls it off. Brave in my growing frenzy, I lean forward to run my mouth over it and hear him grunt with surprised delight.

His skin is so smooth! I haven't been this close to a half-clothed man before and don't know what to expect. My hands run over his warm skin, trying to memorize him, and I offer my mouth again.

He kisses me in response, nudging me back against the pillows as he unbuckles his belt. I sneak a peek as he frees himself and pulls his pants impatiently off his thighs. As he kicks off his pants and the boxers, I wonder if he'll push that big tool into me as soon as my panties are off.

I could almost forgive his being so abrupt. *And I thought this was going to be awkward!* He pulls me up against him, the head of his cock rubbing against me through the silk of my underwear, and hear another grunt of pleasure at the contact.

It's not awkward—I'm too caught up in sensation to care about how I look to anyone but him. And he's so into me that he's shaking.

Talk about a confidence boost. But it's more than that. It's *him.*

His free hand explores me as he crouches naked over me. His smooth hand slides up my hip, over my waist, up my side, then gently cups one of my breasts. "Your skin's so soft," he purrs as he strokes one of my nipples erect with the side of his finger. "I could do this all day."

"I wouldn't c-complain." He starts kissing my neck. He's nibbling and suckling, tiny pricks of pain mixing with my pleasure ... and somehow making it stronger.

Being kissed is usually pleasant, but never in a way that makes me chase after it when it breaks. I've never shivered with anticipation when a man touched my breast instead of being repulsed by an impatient grab.

I've never been given the time to get turned on ... the consideration. Not to mention the someone whose body feels so incredible against mine.

My eyes fly open when his hot breath blows over my nipple and I feel his tongue sliding around the edge of my areola. He goes so slowly, I'm moaning and arching in a wordless plea before his mouth finally closes over me. The first pull of his mouth gets a cry from me as my heels slide against the mattress.

I lose control, stretching under him, panting, gasping, as he sucks almost roughly. His free hand tenderly cradles my breast, holding it in place for his eager mouth. My fingers tangle in his hair; it's so intense for a moment that I want to push him away from me.

Instead, I hold out, moaning with each breath, feeling my cunt tighten and tingle with each pull of his mouth. "Yes," I breathe as he starts rolling my other nipple between his fingers. My hips jolt against his thigh as he suckles. *Yes. Yes. Yes.*

His hand slides behind me, supporting my back as I arch against his mouth. My nipples become two burning points of pleasure, stoked by his hungry suckling until I can't form words any more. By the time he slides off my soaked panties, all I can do is tremble and clutch at him.

The head of his cock is at my entrance and his fingers part me. I jump, panting, then lift my hips welcomingly. His thickness slips into me, and I push up against it.

He thrusts slowly, deliciously stretching open my virgin cunt, the pleasure spiced with bits of pain as my flesh struggles to accommodate him. His back arches as he pushes forward as he groans through his teeth.

"Oh baby ... aah ..." he gasps, and his cock twitches inside me. His voice is breathless with pleasure and, for a disappointed moment, I think he's done. But then he thrusts deeper, panting hard.

He holds still once he's fully inside of me, huffing and shaking, a mist of sweat gleaming on his body. I look past him at my vanity mirror and see him crouched between my thighs, buttocks bunched and back arched as he pushes our hips together. My pussy tightens around him in excitement, but even as I roll my hips to feel him better, I'm still unsatisfied.

There's something more ... something I need, as much as the feel of his cock sliding in and out of me. But for now, being held tight in his arms, feeling him shudder against me and hearing his shallow, desperate pants in my ear, I lay aside my cravings and enjoy his helpless bliss.

"Don't move," he pants. "You feel so fucking good, you'll set me off." He sounds stunned, awed, delighted; his fingernails digging into me.

For a moment, excited and driven half-wild by his caresses, I want to grind on him, just to watch and enjoy what it will do. But then I obey, relaxing as much tension my belly will let me.

"Ahh ... good girl. I haven't gone without a rubber in years." He groans softly, almost like a purr, as my pussy clenches tighter around him in response to his tremors. "Want to take care of you first ..."

He leans on one arm to make space between us, and lays his smooth, nimble hand over my aching vulva. My clit tingles as he starts to knead, stroking it with my own flesh as he holds still inside of me. "Oh yes," I whisper.

"You like that?" he grunts with pleasure as I start squirming under him. My hips rock against his hand; my belly flutters, and the tingling in my clit intensifies as every muscle in my body starts to tighten.

"Oh," I whisper breathlessly as my hips lift against him and my belly tightens almost painfully. "Oh, don't stop ..." My voice stutters as my body starts to tremble.

"I won't," he promises, and smiles down at me tenderly as he kneads and strokes until I'm thrashing and moaning. Each movement makes my clit tingle harder. My muscles are so tight ... it almost hurts ... but I eagerly grind against him as he speeds his movements.

"Come on," he croons as he watches me. His hand moves like a machine, unwavering, firm, his caresses steady as he encourages. I close my eyes—and the sensation rockets toward its peak.

"Daniel," I gasp, almost scared—and then his mouth comes down on mine and muffles my screams.

And scream I do, long wails matching the waves of ecstasy that convulse my body. My fingers dig into his back as I grind against his hand and his cock, hungry for more, adoring him, my screaming slowly settling into long coos of peace.

All through the storm Daniel stiffens and pants for control, gasping with relief as I finally settle down. He relaxes, slowly rolling his hips, and lets out a low, musical moan as he raises his mouth from my lips. "Oh God," he sighs, moving inside of me, and I caress his back as he shivers.

I'm glowing. A soft haze covers the world. He looms over me, his whole body pressing down on me as he thrusts gently.

"It felt so good," I whisper, getting turned on again from the memory. Pleasure so intense it took me over, *he* took me over ... and I couldn't have loved it more. Tears of gratitude run down my face and he leans to kiss them away.

"We're just getting started," he whispers, and then goes to suckle at my breast again.

Time starts to blurring for me. We roll, slide, and stretch over my big mattress, pushing the coverlets and pillows off, stopping here and there to grind together, the heat between us arousing me until I'm trembling and clutching at him wildly again. He fights to hold out, low growls of frustrated pleasure and lust vibrating his chest as he works his hand between us again.

It doesn't take long this time. I'm already turned on, primed, his rough thrusts teasing my sensations to new heights—and I'm eager to feel that again. He obliges, kneading and stroking in time to the beat of his hips.

I croon, rolling my head from side to side and then arching luxuriantly. "Oh yes ... yes ..." The walls of my cunt clench and ripple around his surging cock.

His muscles tighten and he throws his head back, a harsh shout echoing off my bedroom walls, bucking under him uncontrollably—and he pins me in response, thrusting deep.

He pounds away, his roughness only driving more contractions from me as he arches above me. I can hear the slap of our hips meeting; his almost agonized groans growing louder and harsher; the creak of bed springs as he shakes the mattress under us. His cock's slick with my juices now, churning fast in and out of my relaxed body without a hint of pain.

His grip on me tightens almost painfully; he lets out a hoarse "Oh!" and jams his hips against mine. His cock jolts inside of me; a rush of heat each time, and a mix of anguish and delight on his face as he trembles over me, eyes closed.

Finally, he relaxes with a sigh, head drooping.

I remove my fingers from his shoulders, my body limp and tingling. His cock stays firm inside of me. When he opens his eyes, he looks at me. "You okay?"

"I'm really good," I purr, and he smiles.

"Good. Because I'm not done with you yet ..."

My eyes fly open as he grins at me, somewhat tiredly. Then he reaches for me again.

It takes him a while before he can fuck me but he fills that up with sleepy caresses, his long fingers exploring every part of me. His touch is almost reverent until it intensifies as he recovers fully. Soon after, he has me so turned on I can't even form words.

I never knew it could be like this, I think, astonished, a moment before I can't think at all.

Later, completely slack, throat a little sore from my cries of pleasure, I finally hold him as he shudders to a climax a second time. My eyes can't open; I can only feel it as he lies over me and lays his head on my shoulder.

It's done. I'm not a virgin any more.

I literally can't move ... and he can't either, or he doesn't want to. His cock slowly shrinks inside me and another ripple of pleasure runs through me, like an aftershock.

He's collapsed over me, his face turned to the side so I can see the expression of bliss on it. Another faint jolt of pleasure runs through me, along with a strange triumph.

I close my eyes, drifting off blissfully. *I chose right. You are the one.*

But even as I slide into sleep, there's a pang of sadness and regret as he slips out of bed ... and leaves. What it will be like when he leaves for good?

That's a long time away. I turn my face to the pillow.

9

DANIEL

That didn't go as intended. It was fucking amazing ... but I might be in trouble.

It's raining again by the time I can drag myself out of Amelie's bed and put my clothes back on. My legs are wobbly, I'm thirsty and starved ... and yet I'm more relaxed than in years. *Holy crap,* I'm thinking, while pulling my pants back on over tingling skin.

I've done well. She was satisfied in ways any woman in her position would be desperate for. Women like this don't just want a test tube baby.

They want to be fucked properly. Otherwise, why get a stud instead of a lab visit and some handpicked donor? Maybe it's oversimplifying things, but I was right when it comes to Amelie.

She wants more of this. I pull on my shoes and turn to get out of the room. *With enough sex candy and good companionship, she'll fall for me. For certain.*

I step out of the door, quietly close it, and lean against the wall just outside, watching the rain through a hall window, gathering my strength. *I swore to do anything to make up for what my stupidity cost Caroline. Even make a billionaire fall in love with me.*

Whatever else happens, at least Amelie will be distracted and pleased long enough to pay for the surgery, the exoskeleton, and anything else to help Caroline.

There's something else, though; if I get another boner soon, I will be right back in that room and on her in seconds. And she will love it.

And I will love it too.

And that's risky. It's fucking dodgy and you know better.

It's not actually a temptation, not for a while at least. She got everything; light and tingly from knees to belly; I emptied myself in her and enjoyed every second of it. I've never felt this much intensity with a woman, ever!

Even my wife, Mariah, the mother of my child. The woman who took all the light out of my life when she passed.

The years with Mariah were wonderful, loving, and optimistic despite our financial struggles. They were full of her kindnesses. Her past left her sexually shy and I was always tender with her. Despite my enduring love, this level of sheer intoxication was unknown to me before Amelie.

I squeeze my eyes shut. *What the hell is going on?*

The seduction is going perfectly. Amelie is having so much fun, she doesn't want my visit to end. It's only my opening move ... but she's taken to it even more than expected. *But it's supposed to be one-sided.*

My feet need to remain on the goddamn ground to maintain control of this situation. Otherwise it could all come crashing down.

I walk down to the kitchen, enjoying Amelie's scent clinging to my skin. The place is bigger than some restaurant kitchens, with stainless steel and copper counters, a walk-in freezer, and a pantry bigger than the bedroom of my hotel suite. I grab a pitcher of filtered water from the fridge and drain it, glass after thirstily gulped glass, as I create a towering deli sandwich for myself.

Am I dissing Mariah by getting so turned on with another woman? But then I smirk and dismiss the thought. *Holy shit, okay. Stop being emo and get some clarity.*

It was remarkably good sex. I'll be happy to keep having remark-ably good sex with Amelie for the next few months. If it naturally turns into a relationship, all the better—but until the situation is established, I can't fall for her.

Taking a seat at the breakfast table, I take massive bite of my sandwich, chewing rapidly. Lightning flashes outside and the rumble of thunder comes several seconds later.

It will take five to six months before she starts asking why the sex hasn't produced a pregnancy yet. *If she's happy enough, she may not notice or care. But I can't lose my head in the process.*

My phone rings when I'm halfway through the sandwich. Dr. Weiss is calling using the burner phone I gave him. "Afternoon, Doc," I say in a mellow voice, ignoring the apprehension in my gut.

"Good afternoon, Mr. Fontaine. I trust that you and your daughter are properly installed at Ms. LaBelle's mansion?" Weiss has an arch, cold tone to his voice that makes my eyes narrow. I put my sandwich down on the plate.

"Yes, thanks, she's napping. How can I help you today?" I already identify it and the very thought sends my blood pressure rising.

"It's regarding these tests. My career is at risk by falsifying records for you," he says in the same snippy tone, now with an edge of glee.

Oh, you fucker. How much extra is this going to cost? "Go on."

"An additional fifty thousand."

I break into a dry little laugh. "Shit, man, do you have a payment coming up on your yacht or something?" I want to squeeze his fucking neck with both my hands.

"How the bribe money is spent is none of your concern, Mr. Fontaine." His voice gets cold and arrogant. Defensive: the bastard knows he's being greedy.

"And if I say no?" A faint, sharp intake of breath as I challenge him.

"You will have your recent vasectomy exposed and end up jailed for fraud," he says mechanically, as if reading a script. How much time and whiskey did it take this prick to get the nerve to call me?

"Do you really plan to drop the dime when it will implicate you as well, and ruin your career?"

A long silence follows. I smirk and take another bite of my sandwich, chewing while waiting for a reply.

"Those are my terms," he says in the same mechanical tone. There's brittle ego behind it and I smile.

"Look. Doc, you are allotted a fortune to help Amelie get a healthy baby—which she will get, just with some delay. You are also paid to hide my vasectomy for six months or so until it's reversed. By Christmas, she'll have a solid pregnancy, you'll have your cash, and we'll go our separate ways. Why mess with such a good deal?" I ask reasonably.

He's silent again. Savagely, I bite into the sandwich and chew. *Give in, you fucker.*

"I have more money than you and can afford better lawyers," he ventures, and I roll my eyes.

"That's not true any longer, remember?" I gently reply.

He huffs twice and hangs up.

I close my eyes and sigh, trying to control the rush of adrenaline. I don't like being threatened. Or blackmailed!

Fortunately, Weiss doesn't know what he's doing and seems to realize that squeezing me for more cash didn't go as planned. It worries me. Doctors have a superiority complex. It makes them overconfident.

It could mess up all our lives if he fucks up. That would mean jail for me, a broken heart, and lost hope for my daughter. *I will kill that little bastard before that happens.*

Blackmail out of greed escalates as long as the greedy person has something on you. If I encourage him, Weiss will make the same goddamn call every month or so, bleeding me of the money for Caroline's surgery. Now, I've forced him to consider how his plan to "penalize" me will fuck him as well.

Still, his sense of revenge. Doctors hate being outsmarted by anyone who doesn't have letters following their name.

I finish my sandwich, watching the storm, trying to figure out what to do. *Maybe go back to Dr. Parikh, get the gel flushed out, and make a liar out of Weiss before he has the chance to rat on me?*

I take a deep breath as lightning flashes beyond the windows. *That would be easier said than done. Parikh will not be back in town for a few months. Maybe find someone else?*

A faint pang of guilt overcomes me as I rise to put my plate in the sink. *I wish this shit never happened. I'd rather go back to building houses.*

But building houses won't pay enough to treat my daughter, thanks to gluttonous doctors like Weiss. Neither will small investment commissions. My options have been limited since the night my uncle pulled out his car keys and ruined our lives with his lies.

Amelie doesn't have to get hurt. She never has to know. She'll get what she wants, and barely miss the money.

If we get more out of this—if we live here on a permanent basis, me, my wife, and Caroline—it's even better. Either way, I have to pull it off flawlessly—or everything will come crashing down.

Caroline's worth the risk, I remind myself, going back upstairs to check on her.

But that tiny pang of guilt is haunting me.

10

AMELIE

"How long have you been making jewelry?" Caroline asks as I set down my polishing cloth. I've moved my portable worktable out to the screened porch to finish off a few pieces; my workshop sometimes feels claustrophobic when the weather is nice.

Daniel's daughter wheels over. We're fast becoming friends, and I smile at her approach. Especially since she's often exhausted.

Right now, she's somewhat pale but much better; she moved while recovering from her latest surgery. She never did more than quietly complain about pain. She's such a trooper! Daniel shows his pride in her frequently as well.

He's such a good dad. What would it be like if he stuck around ... to be a dad to my child too?

I smile wistfully at nothing and turn my head hastily to answer. "Uh, my grandmother taught me how to knot pearl necklaces when I was sixteen, and it sort of built on that."

It's been a month since they moved into my life and the days have rushed by. I was worried having people in my space would bother me long-term, but it's wonderful! No more loneliness gnawing inside of me—a sensation that has never been comfortable.

"Why do you have to put a knot between each pearl anyway?" She gazes at the amber, jet, and fossil piece I've been polishing. "Is it so they won't slide off if the string breaks?"

"That's part of it. Chasing after lost pearls is not fun. Nothing rolls under furniture faster." I hold up the heavy necklace and watch the cherry amber light up in the sun. "The other reason is that pearls are delicate and the knots keep them from rubbing together and damaging one another."

Her eyes light up. "Oh, so it's like a padding,"

"Exactly. You're quite clever, Caroline. How are you feeling today, anyway?" I set the necklace down.

"Well, it hurts, but it's different. Before, it hurt and I couldn't move that part of my back. Now, I can move it but it hurts lower now." She wiggles, then winces.

"You don't have to show me, honey. I'm sorry it hurts, but did you feel anything there before?"

She shakes her head. "No. And I'd rather hurt for a while than feel nothing at all."

"That's usually best."

"Dad says they'll give me robot pants so I can walk again," she says solemnly and I have to stifle a giggle.

"It's an exoskeleton, sweetheart. You wear it over your pants. Your daddy told me about it." It seems pretty high-tech and amazing. When he first brought it up, I offered to further fund the program.

Taking blood money out of gem mining made me rich. Investing in medical technology to help people walk again is good for my soul.

"How can something like that teach me to walk again?" She tilts her head.

"It is controlled by your thoughts and it moves the legs for you so your muscles and joints remember what walking is like. That way your muscles will stay strong—maybe strong enough that you won't need the exoskeleton one day."

"Will I be able to feel my legs, or just move them?" She looks down at her legs, which are scarred and thin.

"Once you get the last of those bone fragments away from where they're pressing on your spine, you should feel more, if not every-thing." *Am I explaining this well?*

Living with Caroline has been a crash course in living with a kid. She's smarter and more mature than most nine-year-olds, but she's still a kid and sometimes my inexperience with children really shows. She's always asking what the ten-dollar word I just used means, for example.

She's adjusting, but I could do so more myself. I don't want to upset her. She's had a very rough time and I care about her.

Besides, her daddy dotes on her, and anything that might drive him away is the last thing on my mind.

That man is candy. I can't get enough. And even though he's being paid, nobody pays him to spoil me like this.

Before him, I had never had sex. I never knew what it felt like to be fully turned on. Now, I don't fall asleep without sinking into that wonderful, soft feeling of satisfaction that comes after I do.

Cock, fingers, tongue ... the man works hard to drive me wild and turn sex into a treat. So I want to keep him happy.

"What's the hardest part of jewelry making?" Caroline peers at the necklace but is thoughtful enough not to touch.

"Most jewelry is made of metal, and metals are tough to work with. You have to use smelly fluxes and polishes, heat them up, and bang on them, all kinds of things. It's fun to see it come together, but it's stinky and hard on the hands."

"Sounds like physical therapy," she sighs.

"But the docs say you're doing much better," I remind her.

"Yeah. I just get frustrated sometimes," she admits. "When you're doing the exercises, it's all boring. And I still hurt. But reading my journal, it used to hurt much worse."

I nod, my smile frozen on my face. *She should never have gone through this. But here she is, toughing her way through with barely a complaint.*

"Are you and Dad getting along?" she asks. I blink, yanked out of my line of thinking.

"Okay?" *Last night we made love three times, once in the garden gazebo, once in the shower, and once in bed. I came until I cried. But you don't need to know about any of that, honey.* "Um, everything's great. Why do you ask?"

"I know it's selfish," she replies a little sadly. "But I don't want to leave again. We're always changing where we live. And I hate hotels!"

"Oh, don't worry about that," I reassure her at once, trying to push the memory of her dad pinning me to the shower wall out of my head before blurting something embarrassing out. "I enjoy the company."

Caroline smiles and relaxes a little. I smile back and return to work, answering her bright questions as I go.

Dr. Weiss is strangely cold and short at my checkup. His mouth is a line and his normally pleasant demeanor is subdued. Is he feeling well?

"No signs of pregnancy yet, I'm afraid," he says apologetically. "Any changes in your menstruation?"

"It's been a bit erratic. I assumed it was from stress." He nods.

"It might well be. I suggest you boost your intake of broad-spectrum B vitamins and D. And try to get more sleep. Have you cut back on work hours?" He's taking notes on his pad, occasionally glancing at me.

Why do his eyes look so cold?

"I'll do that." It's only been a month and a half. There are a dozen reasons to keep Daniel and his daughter around, at least through Christmas. Even if there's no bun in the oven yet.

Besides, these things often take time. A few of my girlfriends took years before they managed a successful pregnancy. And it's not a problem having Daniel and his daughter around.

Quite the contrary. In spite of that, it troubles me now and makes me wonder if things will work. Maybe it's not about a pregnancy.

It's my fertility specialist's odd manner. "Is something wrong, Dr. Weiss?"

He stares at me for several moments, as if considering something. Then he pulls the corners of his mouth in a fake smile and says, "No, not at all. Have a good day, Ms. LaBelle."

Daniel is congenially chatting with Weiss's aging, sweet-faced receptionist when I come out. About his daughter, of course. "Yes, she's strong enough now to do physical therapy daily and she has more mobility in her back."

The receptionist beams. "She'll always be in my prayers. But here's your wife now. You two have a lovely day!"

She has no idea of our true relationship and I feel a strange reluctance to correct her. "Thanks so much. You too!" I reply as Daniel offers me his arm.

"How did it go?" Daniel asks quietly as we walk out.

"Nothing yet, but that's not really a surprise. It's only been six weeks, after all." I keep my voice light. In the back of my head, I am wondering why Dr. Weiss glared and scowled his way through the entire exam.

"We're both healthy, so it shouldn't take forever. Making a baby can actually take a fairly long time. It took us about six months to conceive Caroline." His hand brushes mine and I take it almost reflexively.

"You're likely right. I'll worry more about it in a few months." I am realizing that having a baby and raising a child is complicated ... and I am also not eager for Daniel to leave.

There is a look of relief in his eyes as he steps forward to unlock the car door for me.

11

DANIEL

Spring is here and with it, another surgery. Caroline has less pain with each week that goes by. It's not just the surgeries and physical therapy now. It's living somewhere where she can roll around, be in the sun, swim, and not be someplace that reminds her of our desperate days.

She's happy now. She wakes up smiling each morning.

Amelie is doing well too. From fucking her silly at every opportunity, to catching her up on all the movies and shows and things around town she's missed by being a reclusive workaholic, it's certain that she's happy. I don't know if she's fallen for me yet, but that dewy-eyed look she gives me after she climaxes reassures me she won't give it up easily.

As for me ... well, I'm a wreck. But a productive wreck, and they're both happy, so something is going right.

"Do you want me to come with you?" Amelie asks over breakfast. She knows me too well already. Every time my little girl goes under the knife, it wrecks my nerves and she can tell.

It's no big deal. It's my worry to wrestle with and she's getting too far under my skin as it is.

Even Caroline is calm about the surgery. She's gotten experienced at this: always my little hero. I'm just pretending.

I'm used to doing it by myself and have no business leaning on Amelie—especially with what I'm doing to her.

"Sure, if you don't mind." *Why the fuck did I say that?*

But that's just ... how it's going for me lately. Amelie may not have fallen for me yet, but I'm fighting not to fall for her. I doubt it'll succeed.

"No problem," she replies, smiling softly.

Caroline is sleeping later; she can't eat before her surgery. I busy myself with huevos rancheros while trying to sort out my thoughts. That, and the goddamn guilt from every single time Amelie does something kind that I don't fucking deserve.

I got into this supposing she was a typical billionaire with a touch more ethics. It's true she will barely miss the money. But she never deserved to be the target of a con.

Amelie seems to disprove every assumption I've ever made about her. From her heartbreaking loneliness to her genuine kindness, she's more than big-hearted in that "I'm rich and afford to be generous" way. She cares about people, even though so many of them have been rotten to her.

The more she does that, and the more attached I get to her, the more like a piece of shit I feel. Here I am lying and hiding the fact I'm on birth control to draw out time with her ... and yet I'm learning she would probably help us anyhow.

Jesus, I'm a goddamn heel.

"Is something wrong?" she asks me softly.

"You know, you don't have to care so much."

She looks hurt, and I start to suspect how attached she's gotten. It should make me feel triumphant: another hint I've won her heart. Instead it makes me feel even worse.

"Sorry, does it bother you?" she asks in a smaller voice.

I look at her, and then smile wryly. "Bother? No. It's flattering. You're the one who keeps saying this whole arrangement is business —no matter how amazing the sex is."

My eyebrows bounce on the last bit, and I don't hide the gleam in my eyes. Sex with her is more than amazing. It's next level. I exhaust myself with her every chance possible.

She smiles and blushes, looking at the table. "So we can't be friends then? The contract you signed did not say a thing about that."

"I just don't want to disappoint you." What she doesn't know can't hurt her ... but every damn day that goes by chews holes in me.

I fucking deserve this. But if I stop now ... as soon as she gets a positive pregnancy test, my job's done. And with it my chance to make sure my daughter gets everything she needs.

I never wanted to be a fucking criminal in the first place. But like this job—the last job, it's all been forced on me. It was either this, or Caroline suffering for the rest of her life.

Because of her dead piece-of-shit great uncle and because of me.

Amelie scoffs. "Disappoint me? So far you've done the opposite at every turn."

"That's good to hear. And indeed, nothing in the paperwork says we can't be friends. Hell, it's probably better if we are." I smile charmingly and drop the subject, and eat my breakfast, not tasting a single bite.

"There are currently three bone fragments remaining pressing against your daughter's spinal cord. The cord was not severed; instead, it has been severely pinched. As we previously discussed, it's partial spinal damage." Dr. Bryant is a small, birdlike woman with fluffy gray-blonde hair cut to jaw-length, currently twittering information to me from behind her big steel boat of a desk.

"This is why she has bladder and bowel control and has regained some sensation. We don't know how much control of her legs she will have by removing the fragments. However, if her progress continues as it has in the last eighteen months, chances are she'll eventually graduate to a cane."

Not good enough. "Thank you, Doctor," I say with a smile. "So how many of the slivers will be removed today?"

I spent fifteen minutes before this meeting calming Caroline down and holding her hand as she drifted off from the anesthetics.

The whole time, she actually seemed calmer than I was inside. Watching her prepped for surgery always makes my stomach feel like a million crickets are jumping around inside.

I stayed tough for her; I always do. But the doctor's last-minute briefings, though well-intentioned and more information than other doctors give, aren't fun to sit through. It would help if I wasn't so fucking imaginative; I've been to bloody surgeries before but it's never amusing thinking of someone cutting into your child's back.

"Two are close to one another. We'll be able to remove them with retractors and a laparoscope. The third will require a final surgery. Otherwise we'll have to make a larger incision, which means keeping her up to a week and potentially losing progress on her rehabilitation."

I sigh. "What about the exoskeleton?"

"Not my department, although our prosthesis expert has done some research. Your specialist, Dr. Grace, should be returning in mid-July, in time so Caroline recovers from the last surgery."

She smiles almost mechanically. "Of course, by then we'll be running into summer vacation. He may want to delay."

I exchange glances with Amelie, who has been sitting quietly beside me. She's the one insisting on writing the check, so it's her concern too.

"Does Dr. Grace have a forwarding number?" she speaks up suddenly. She has her cool, all-business tone and the doctor straightens up and looks at her.

"He does, if you wish to discuss faster arrangements." She starts fishing in her desk drawer for a card as Amelie nods.

"I can make a deal to get her completely fitted before the end of the year. I can certainly make it worth his while."

She looks so cool, so perfect, so in control—and it's making my cock hard despite the stress. I love it when she shows her power. The fact she's doing it like a mother lioness for my little girl just makes me crave her more.

I don't deserve her. But the desire's winning, and soon that thought floats out of my fevered mind.

"All right." The doctor closes her laptop and gives Amelie a business card. "Caroline's anesthesia has taken hold and she's being monitored. I need to go to her ward and scrub down. I'll see you with a report in half an hour."

The reality of Caroline's surgery comes back like a splash of cold water in my face. I stand up and Amelie rises beside me. "Of course, Doctor. Thank you."

"What will you do if she doesn't regain full sensation in her legs?" Amelie asks me gently as we drive home two hours later.

"Keep looking for a medical procedure that works, regardless of how long it takes." I can't keep the grimness out of my voice. "She'll walk again, no matter what it costs me or what I have to do."

She's looking at me tenderly. I can't meet her eyes. "Let me help," she gently requests. I pull the car over and close my eyes to think.

Say yes for Caroline's sake. You might be able to do it on your own but Amelie can get it done faster.

"I'm not asking for a savior," I protest. The honest truth slips out before I can stop it. "I don't deserve you swooping in. The bonus you've offered is enough."

She sighs through her nose and lifts her chin, and the firmness in her voice cuts through the conflict in my head. "Whether or not you deserve my help doesn't figure in here. Caroline does. My father was a rotten man, all right? He spent money on whores he brought home and was too busy drinking to maintain the domicile or manage his money. I inherited what he had left— and multiplied it tenfold in three years. I've already made my first five billion, Daniel. What the hell is the point of all this money if I can't do something good?" She sounds troubled and determined.

Oh man. She's twisting the knife and doesn't even know it. "I'm flattered you trust me. But you already do a lot of good, okay?"

She gives me an anxious glance as we move back into the congested traffic. "I know you're the only gem and gold mine to maintain international safety and pollution standards and pay a living wage. You regularly get people out of debt. You do enough as it is."

And I really don't deserve your help. I've kept the contraceptive gels instead of having them flushed out because I worried she would quickly conceive and decide to be rid of me.

It was a con in the first place. Can I fix that or make up for it now? Focusing on the road, I fight the urge to say more.

"Let me do this," she asks almost pleadingly. "Money can't fix everything, but at least I can get an exoskeleton from your specialist by Christmas."

My heart is beating fast. She's reached out with a soft finger and touched the raw muscle as it pulses in my chest: pain and warmth— and more vulnerability. "Let's see how much Caroline improves after this surgery and then talk about it."

She seems satisfied with that. "What time can we pick up Caroline?"

"She came through surgery but they will keep her overnight. Tomorrow around ten." I won't sleep.

I never sleep when my little girl is not home and well. It's not very logical, especially knowing she's in good hands.

At the bottom of the off-ramp I slow down for cross traffic— and as the truck comes to a stop, Amelie's slim, soft hand touches on my arm.

"Stay with me tonight?"

The surprise makes me glad the car's not moving. My cock goes so hard it hurts, and I turn to look at her.

There's heat in her eyes, behind the demure curtain of her lashes.

I should say no. But I answer with a kiss.

We're all over each other as soon as we get home and upstairs. We don't even speak beyond what it takes for her to lead me by the hand into her room. Then she turns to me, and we kiss like we're both desperate.

Maybe I am. My body shakes, my cock throbs impatiently, and I have to fight myself to keep from bruising her with a too-enthusiastic grip.

I don't want to think anymore. Caroline got through the surgery. The worry, the guilt, the stormy emotions ... I need them out of my head.

I wrap myself up in Amelie and pray that I won't feel or think at all outside of my time in her arms soon enough.

Her skin is so responsive, so smooth. Nibbling at the base of her spine makes her moan. It doesn't take much before she's panting. I've had enough time to learn her body; to learn what pleases her.

When I'm tender, she cries and clings to me. Her climaxes come slow and long, like ripples across a pond. Then I explode from holding out.

When I'm rough, she pushes back, fierce, hungry for me, nails in my skin. I proudly wear the marks the next day, remembering her cries and pleas for more. Her last climax carries me with it every time.

Sometimes we go at it until we both wear out and wake up hours later still in each other's arms. I usually wake up first and watch her sleep until the shame hits. Then I clean up and dress, and leave her alone.

I'm still a cock for hire who isn't giving her the baby she wants quite yet—but now that she's offering to help us anyway, I have no reason to hold out anymore.

It's fully realized this time as I fuck her facing the vanity mirror—she on all fours over a mound of pillows and me kneeling behind her, thrusting slowly as I watch her. Her eyes are closed in bliss as I meet my own gaze in the mirror.

I keep thrusting, my hand at work against her wet, swollen pussy, making her moan ... I can barely enjoy it. My heart is too heavy. If it wasn't Amelie, I probably wouldn't be hard at all.

The guilt won't go away. Neither will the risk of Weiss's betrayal. *I'll making an appointment with a urologist later today and give the lady what she paid for.*

Only then can I finally relax enough to let pleasure take over.

I caress her gorgeous, thick ass as I slap my hips against it, grunting with every time I sink my shaft into her. Her hot, slick cunt tightens on me as I slide in fully, and she gasps in response, squirming against me.

Her brown eyes squint and her head falls back as she arches. I run my fingers through her soft brown curls, tugging firmly before caressing her and letting my hand slide down her back. She purrs, rolling her ass against me.

Her climax makes her moan into the mound of pillows; I thrust harder, excited by her cries and movements. For a few moments, a wild mix of lust and ecstasy overcomes me—and then my release whites out my mind.

I come to, draped over her, and carefully back off as she rolls onto her side with a sigh. I get off the bed and lay a blanket over her, my legs wobbly but my mind clear.

I grab the phone from my jeans while heading to the bathroom. *She promised to get Caroline an exoskeleton by Christmas. She'll have a baby in her belly by then too.*

Once my goddamn part is done, maybe I can live with myself again.

12

AMELIE

It's been four months and I'm not pregnant yet, which makes me worry. Dr. Weiss said there's no problem with my reproductive system, or with Daniel's ... but something has been nagging at me.

Daniel and I make love every night and at every opportunity during the day. Yet every month, my period comes like clockwork. If the information Weiss gave me is correct, this shouldn't be.

But Weiss has been acting strangely for months ... and I never got a second opinion. *Maybe it's time*. I shower alone after my latest round with Daniel.

Weiss has an impeccable reputation, and I pay him a lot. But he's very wealthy and very ... distant for a man who helps women conceive, and ... reputations can be bought.

I could accept the delay for more time with Daniel. If trouble conceiving equals more months of being exquisitely boned every night by that amazing man, I'll take it. But that's not what bothers me.

Something isn't adding up. I've felt it since Weiss's shift in manner. Can I trust him?

My hands smooth down my belly, which Daniel likes to kiss. A smile ghosts onto my face. It's been amazing ... transformative.

Don't watch him walk away.

Couldn't I ask him to stay? To start a relationship, like normal people? We work together. Everyone's happy.

Leaning against the cool shower wall, the hot water sprinkles over me, and my stomach suddenly tightens. *That wasn't the deal. He's supposed to provide me with a baby, not become my new man.*

What if he's not interested in something deeper? Is he on his best behavior to get the job done? Will it get worse if he stays?

A huge lump in my throat goes down as I dry off. My eyes are stinging. I don't know which is worse: Daniel leaving, or finding out that Daniel is just like all the rest.

What to do? I grab a chicken sandwich and some sweet tea. Finally, I give up and focus on more practical things. Like how all that dazzling, amazing sex somehow hasn't produced a pregnancy.

It can't be our fault. No doctor has ever told me I have signs of fertility problems and Daniel has a daughter. Unless Weiss missed something ... which I'm starting to suspect.

I take a bite of the sandwich, getting my irritation under control. Doctors are only human. There's plenty of time to fix this.

Another doctor should examine Daniel to be certain.

Dr. Weiss can transfer my records to the other specialist. After voicing my request, his receptionist puts me on hold for almost ten minutes. When the line picks back up, it's Weiss himself.

"May I help you, Ms. LaBelle?" he asks with a suspicious edge.

"Yes, I want a copy of my medical records. My electronic signature is on a permission sheet and the records can be released. It's a common request." Why is he acting like this? The discomfort is in my voice.

There's a long pause. "... Of course. My receptionist must have misunderstood your request." His voice sounds more measured. That's more suspicious!

"There's no problem then?" I ask in my businesslike tone. *Fuck you, Weiss.*

"None at all," he says hastily. "Why are you requesting the records now?"

"Insurance reimbursement," I lie smoothly. "They're giving me static on covering my fertility counseling."

"Oh!" Now he sounds relieved and now I'm really worried. "Of course. I'll have them faxed over right away."

"Damn it," I mutter after he hangs up. My heart is nervously banging away in my chest. "What are you hiding, Weiss?"

The time dealing with my father has left me with an instinct for slimy men. To detect male lies and avoidance in general. Daniel for example is tight-lipped about many things, but his motives—and passion for me—are obvious and can hardly be judged as terrible.

But after four months, a paranoid doctor who guarantees our fertility aren't playing out. A doctor who gets nervous about copies of my records... After every damn thing I have been through, Dr. Weiss is setting off more alarm bells than a warehouse fire.

I tiredly rub my temples, staring at the screen of my smartphone. I need to discuss this with Daniel. If something is wrong, will he be all right with going the IVF route?

I still want to have his child, even if Weiss has been tricking us and there is a fertility problem. But going to him with those serious words, "We need to talk" ...

We're not a couple ... even if I wish we could be. No damn business dragging him into relationship conversations. Looks like, soon, there may be no other choice.

"I'm going to talk to another fertility doctor," I tell Daniel as we drive to pick up Caroline.

He looks at me sharply for a split second before focusing back on the road. "Why, is something wrong?"

"With Dr. Weiss, yes." I sense his tension and wish we didn't need this conversation. "He's been behaving suspiciously since my two-month checkup and when I tried to get a copy of my medical records for my insurance, he reacted defensively."

"Fuck," he mutters. "That's not a good sign. Have you been taking any medications prescribed by him?"

"No. Just some vitamin supplements. He said it had to be a year before I could consider fertility drugs. There's always in vitro but ..." I hesitate. "How would you feel about that?"

"It would be fine with me." he says, so quickly it shocks me. He smiles tightly. "I'm paid to get you pregnant, after all."

"That could involve, uh ... needles." Most men seem to balk at the prospect of anything sharp or pointy heading for their sensitive parts.

He scoffs. "One million dollars is enough for a few hours of sore balls. And we're not there yet. So what's your plan?"

He shocks me again, in the most pleasant of ways—just rolling with what's going on instead of balking. "I'll find another fertility specialist to get a second opinion. It shouldn't take long, but you should know ahead of time."

"Okay. Give me the day and time when I'm not driving, so I can put it in my phone." He seems calm, completely in control, surprising me with how flexible he's being. I'm starting to feel better, but then he runs a red light.

Tires screech and honks erupt on either side of us; he realizes too late what he just did and quickly steers through the intersection to get out of everyone's way. Fortunately, it's a sleepy afternoon and the traffic is thin; we're fine, even if I want to smack him.

"Holy crap, Daniel, didn't you notice—" I come out of my anger.

He has wide eyes and a pale face. "I'm sorry," he gasps, and pulls to the side of the street to compose himself. "I'm not sure what just happened."

This is the first time I've seen him mess up. Normally he's dead on. "Do you want me to drive?"

Daniel is a proud man. He opens his mouth to dismiss my concern ... and then closes it, looking thoughtful. Perhaps he remembers his uncle's hideous mistake in driving when he shouldn't have.

"Yes, let's switch. Sorry." He gives me a sheepish grin. "Don't think I'll be myself until Caroline's back home."

I nod and smile. He didn't sleep a wink, and not just because we were making a lot of love through the night. "Let's get there and bring her back. Then we could probably all use a nap."

"Yeah." He looks a little pale. But that is understandable. Still ... I can't shake a sense of worry while driving us to the hospital.

13

DANIEL

Amelie carefully drives us back home, not mentioning the collision my distracted ass almost got us in. I was smarter than my uncle and gave up the keys when I knew I was too distracted to drive. At least it didn't happen when my daughter was in the vehicle. She would have freaked out and left me feeling guiltier.

That didn't happen—just a near miss, and maybe one looming. I sit in the back holding sleepy, sore Caroline, who wears a calm smile that I mirror, brooding behind it.

... *Fuck. Amelie wants a second opinion.* That means either bribe another doctor or come clean before this gets messier.

Or find a way to get my damn tubes flushed ahead of time. No more gel and instantly my sperm count will be normal again. It's only a short procedure and sore balls for the day.

Where's a urologist who will work fast? It's an outpatient procedure that takes less than fifteen minutes. The only problem is, the procedure, like the gel itself, isn't well known in the States yet.

Now I have to slip out of this mess before both of the ladies in my life end up hurt and disappointed. There's no goddamned way Caroline will not be affected by this.

It will kill me if she's disappointed. Also, it will kill me to disappoint Amelie too.

When did that happen? I liked her enough to feel in the wrong within a few days of meeting her. But day by day, week by week, month by month, I've actively tried not to get emotionally involved.

Caroline's attached to her, too, and Amelie clearly cares for her. Over time, we've naturally grown together. I could enjoy it all with a clear conscience and no fear of it falling apart if I had come here honestly.

Now the whole stupid, irrelevant plan that brought me here needs to be fixed before anyone finds out. There is no choice. Otherwise ...

... Fuck. I don't even want to think about it.

We have sherbet on the balcony with Caroline when we get her home. She's tired but more tired of lying in bed.

She slowly eats the sherbet, still queasy from the sedatives. "They say we won't know how well it worked until the swelling goes down. It must have helped because my toes are prickling."

My spoon drops as Amelie and I swap excited looks. *Holy shit. She's feeling something this soon?*

"That's wonderful, sweetheart. I hope it doesn't feel too odd." My smile's genuine for the moment.

She shakes her head and smiles around a mouthful of sherbet. After she pulls out the spoon and swallows, she simply says, "I'll take it."

Amelie beams across the table and I nod. "Me too."

Caroline falls asleep in her chair a while after emptying her bowl. I carry her up to bed and get her settled. When I get back downstairs, Amelie is hanging up her phone with an odd frown.

"Is everything all right?" I ask, on high alert inside and mildly concerned.

"That was Dr. Weiss." My stomach tightens. "He was asking about the records and started rambling. I think he might have been drunk."

Oh, you weak son of a bitch, what did you do? This is why I hate drunks.

I stare at her for several heartbeats before blinking and then saying, "That's really bizarre. Did you ever get the files he was balking at sending?"

"They sent them, but they don't look like a complete copy." The frown on her face makes me sick. "I don't know what to make of this."

Fuck, Weiss, you complete goddamned idiot. If I had known you had no balls before I let you near my own ... "Okay," I put my hands on her shoulders comfortingly.

"Look, we're dealing with two separate problems. Weiss may be a quack, and you're not pregnant yet. We can't control what Weiss does until we level some charges or a lawsuit against him." Do not ask what exactly he said!

Instead, I focus on what Amelie needs and how to help her. Seeing the stress start to leave her makes my gut stop churning on its own.

"Okay, you're right about that part, though I'm tempted to block his number." She rubs her temple, the corner of her mouth tucking up when she tries to force a smile.

"Do that if he starts harassing you, or just hand him to me. I have experience dealing with rich, drunk assholes. Who do you think does the most investing? It's how they gamble." I stroke her hair with my hand and rest it on her shoulder again.

She thinly smiles but at least it's genuine. "Okay, you can run interference. Get as much information on what's going on with him out of him, ASAP."

I nod. "Will do."

"So ... what should we do instead?" We turn and walk, not toward her bedroom but to the sitting room nearby. We settle on its over-stuffed burgundy-and-gold couch and she nestles into my arms.

"The real issue is I still need to give you a baby. It's been months, and you've helped us a lot. I couldn't be more grateful, especially now that Caroline's starting to feel her feet." That's with my full sincerity —even feeling undeserving to have her in my arms.

"This could mean starting from scratch with another doctor. Is there something wrong with my body? I could be barren. I—" She takes a huge breath and I hug her tightly.

"Look, if anyone has a problem, it's me. I was in a big car accident. Snapped both of my femurs almost at hip level. Titanium is a part of me now."

I'll take the blame for this, even without giving up the details. I owe her that. "You are fine. You have periods like clockwork; no other doctor's ever said a thing about fertility problems. I may have scar tissue or something."

She takes a deep breath. "So if we go to this doctor and there's a problem, and we have to do in vitro, with sperm retrieval, you're game for that?"

This time I take a deep breath. That would neatly get around my sperm-blocked vas deferens with nobody the wiser. "Sweetheart, as much as I'd love to stay with you for as long as you'll have me, and Caroline loves it here, if you want the job finished, that's fine.

"In fact, if you tell me you want a sperm retrieval later today, I will do it."

... And more truth spills out again. *Holy shit.*

I freeze up for a moment, then force myself to speak again. "You'll have your pregnancy, and Dr. Weiss's bullshit will have just cost you little time."

She stares at me. For the first time, it's tough to figure out what's going on behind those soft, golden-brown eyes. Maybe the mix of emotions is too complex? Or is it astonishment because she's learned I'd love to stay with her?

"Look, could you answer three of my questions honestly?" she asks. She's trying to be all business but there's vulnerability behind it.

"Proceed," I force out, my heart hammering.

"You really would do a sperm retrieval if needed to prevent further delays?" She's skeptical and incredulous.

I look her in the eye, "Say the word." *Give me a chance to make up for my screw-up without you or my daughter finding out what a lying idiot I am.*

She nods once, and relaxes a little more. "Okay. Next question. You told me everything you receive goes to Caroline's surgeries."

"Every bit. In fact, if you hadn't helped us it wouldn't go far enough. But yeah, that's the bottom line—I'm giving you a baby so my baby can walk again." Still nothing but truth.

She relaxes some more. "Okay. Last question."

This time she hesitates, drawing it out, looking past me, out the window. It makes me hitch my breath and brace myself for her to ask about Weiss.

"Would you really ... want to stay?" Her voice is hopeful and vulnerable, and suddenly I'm aching all through myself and gathering her onto my lap, burying my face in her hair.

"I'm not even fucking sure I deserve you. I'm not perfect. Hell, I almost got us into a car accident earlier today. You deserve a man who is never ashamed of his past, or have something to hide from people." Like turning into a con artist who targets rich people so a bunch of greedy doctors will put my daughter's spine back together.

"I ..." There are tears in her eyes and she pulls away slightly. "Nobody is perfect. How bad is it?"

"Where to begin? I never hurt anyone, outside of kicking my uncle's ass during his arrest. But ..." I hesitate. *Maybe I really should just tell her.*

"How far would you go to make sure your child could walk again?" I breathe out.

She nods gravely, not blinking. "Pretty fucking far. But even then, you'd have ethics. Things you wouldn't do."

There's relief in her face when I say, "Yes. I don't want to be the guy who you can't trust." Even though I have been. How fucking stupid was that?

"I want to be the man you can rely on. The man you deserve." Everything I'm saying is heartfelt but it sounds like fucking drivel and who knows what she's thinking.

"That's nice to hear but ... I've heard a lot of promises from a lot of men. You are the only one to get this close, but words aren't shit without action." Her voice ebbs back and forth between tender and firm and I feel her inside again, this time worse, like she's gripping my heart.

"I will never hurt you," I say quietly. "Not intentionally. Maybe by being a dumbass, but I try not to be."

She lets out a sad laugh. "That puts you a cut above a lot of guys, that's for sure. But ... only proving that makes it real."

I'm such an idiot. "I'm prepared to."

Is it possible to actually make my way out of this and somehow win this magnificent woman? I can't change the cowardice that kept me from fixing this sooner. Can I make up for it?

"Is there anything else?" In some ways, it feels like the hard part's over. Even if I just made an idiot of myself.

She stares at me a long time. It's tough not to look away.

"No," she says gently. "You've already given me a lot to think about. I need a nap now, though."

I cover her up with a blanket and kiss her. *No, I have to fix this!*

The rest of my afternoon is spent calling every urologist in the county to get an appointment in the next two days. Most won't even see me, and the rest balk about the gel since they haven't dealt with it. Dr. Parikh, who injected the stuff in the first place, is still out of town and no way I'm asking Weiss.

I agreed to going ahead with IVF, even if sperm retrieval gets difficult. That can happen without the new doctor ever detecting the gel implants. They're unusual outside of India right now.

They could assume scar tissue is the culprit, narrowing all the little tubes and such so the sperm can't get through. Either way, it would bypass the birth control too. It should work.

That doesn't change the fact that I sailed in here to deceive Amelie and seduce her into keeping me. This was a con. Then I fell for her. I would fucking deserve it if she found out and threw me out.

But Caroline doesn't need to suffer alongside me. Too much of that already.

I start to call more urologists but then stop. Suddenly, I feel like a coward for scrambling for covering my ass.

Amelie will get what she wants. I'll go directly to the retrieval after the sperm test shows a zero count. If the specialist discovers the implants, I'll face the fucking music and beg Amelie to show Caroline some mercy.

I don't deserve any.

14

AMELIE

Daniel's going through with IVF at my request. I am getting what I want, without more fruitless waiting. I should be happy.

My head is spinning as I lie on my bed, cold tears in the corners of my eyes. Pretending to be tired, I sent him away to settle before his touch intoxicates me again. It's not going well.

If what Weiss told me is true, I'm still getting what I want. I'll be pregnant by Christmas by the man I chose.

But I can't be happy about it.

Weiss's phone call—his story—happened as Daniel was putting his daughter to bed. I was tired and worried about the near-accident. Also looking forward to spending half of the afternoon in his arms.

It took me all this time to realize I've fallen for him. I was debating to tell him today. That's what made his affirmation that the feeling's mutual so agonizing ... and so screwed up.

"Shut up and listen," Weiss told me, slurring and snarling. He started to spill out a story that sounded so crazy, he could have made it up. Some of the facts are true and it scares the hell out of me.

"He had a vasectomy. He's been lying to you all along, the bum, so he and his crippled daughter can have a nice place to stay and get the surgeries. He paid me hide his zero sperm count.

"Why did he figure this lie would last forever? If you're planning action against me, better put the blame on the right guy. This was his idea!"

Afterward, in Daniel's arms as he tried to comfort me from pain he may have caused, I thought about the four months it's taken me to get pregnant and tried to figure out whether I can trust him. Instead, I got a confession of love.

Oh God.

He admitted to being imperfect and ashamed of his past. He wanted to do better—and agreed to get me pregnant.

But if Weiss is correct, he fucking lied to me.

"Of course I'm coming home, baby doll. Your momma's just nervous. It's all right." Daddy's silhouette in the dark; an empty shape making empty promises.

Did some fucked-up part of my subconscious make me attracted to another lying scumbag? Do I just draw them, like sharks?

Or is Weiss lying because he's a drunk asshole who resents that I'm checking up on his work and who is trying to distract me with drama to cover his butt?

I have never felt so conflicted; it feels like two angry snakes are warring inside of my gut. And no idea weighing in my head does anything to resolve it.

Get rid of him. He's been lying and tricking me. It's time to regain control before he starts manipulating again.

Forgive him. He's desperate. He's only doing this for his daughter.

I can't trust him. But I can't throw his daughter out when she's depending on me or help. She'll be crushed.

Even if Weiss is telling the truth ... Caroline is Daniel's reason for everything.

How far would you go?

Would you do the wrong thing for the right reasons?

If he's deceiving me, even if he has fallen for me, accepting it means he'll think he can keep lying. I can't live with that.

With the back of my hand, I wipe some tears away. *This is why I stopped dating.* Except this time ... it hurts, because the bastard made me love and crave him before the bomb dropped.

He took my fucking virginity. What can I do if he's just another prick?

I squeeze my eyes. "Stop," I whisper into the pillow, the weakest order. "Stop it. Be objective."

I roll over and stare at the stamped ceiling of my bedroom. How many times has that view blurred before my eyes while Daniel brought me to ecstasy? How many times has it framed his face as he smiled at me?

Do I really want to give that up?

But how can I enjoy it, now that Weiss has planted this seed of doubt?

If I let Weiss ruin everything, my heart will dry up. I'll get sperm from a lab, and my daughter will grow up never trusting men.

But if Daniel really has been lying, even if now his head is out of his ass and is trying to fix it, I can't let it slide either. If I'm not doing a dramatic breakup that will disrupt our lives, I have to find another way to address it.

Wiping my eyes, I walk to my vanity mirror and stare into my face, seeing the streaks of dry tears and the resolve. I won't end up like my mother, trapped in a relationship with a man because of a needy child and the one thing he brought to the table.

What does Daniel bring to the table?

He could lie about loving me! But every damn time he gets emotional, he falls all over himself, like he wasn't expecting it. I doubt he's lying about his feelings for me.

I go into the bathroom and clean myself up. I brush out my hair and catch it behind with a golden clip. *What else?*

Sex, I could never get tired of. Good company—if he doesn't drive distracted. A child who already feels like she belongs here ... and whom I would miss.

I wash the tear streaks off my face and reapply my makeup. My eyeliner is blue. My lips are crimson.

I'm not shaking anymore.

What are Daniel's drawbacks?

He may have lied to me for months! He admitted to having a past he's somewhat ashamed of. He may be infertile and hiding it.

But he's willing to face surgical intervention and recovery to provide me with what he's promised. Which is pretty ballsy, pun intended, and shows commitment.

He may even be completely innocent, in which case I have to plan my response so an undeserving person is not hurt. Maybe there's a way to do this so, if he's done nothing, he'll just end up confused.

If he's been swindling me after all, I need to make sure nothing like this ever happens again. And if that means being a bitch to get that job done ... well ... I didn't make my first billion by being nice.

A smile crosses my freshly-reddened lips as a plan starts to form.

15

DANIEL

"So." I take a deep breath and face my daughter. "It's time I come clean about something."

Amelie and Caroline look at me, leaving me wondering if Amelie's expecting a confession too. How much has Weiss told her? How much does she believe? Amelie has insisted about being honest with my daughter about what's going on, and I'm biting the bullet and doing it.

Later this evening, I'll bite another bullet entirely. Because, to my astonishment, Amelie made an appointment with a world-renowned IVF and sperm retrieval specialist just thirty minutes away ... same day.

She can wield power when she wants to and it has left me a bit intimidated. Especially since, this time, it involves her holding me to my word in a very immediate way. Off we go to the IVF clinic to have my semen tested and then go through a sperm retrieval.

And, of course, pray the exam doesn't reveal the gel.

I'm going to ask for a sedative.

"I didn't come here because Amelie hired me for investments." I try to ignore the heat creeping up the back of my neck. "She hired me to give her a baby."

Caroline blinks at me "Uh ... what?"

... *Fuck*. "There's a place called an IVF clinic where women can get pregnant. Sometimes they hire men to help them."

She scoffs slightly. "I know what sex is, Dad."

Amelie stifles a cough in her handkerchief and I ignore the urge to change the subject to literally anything else. "Uh ... I think you've got the wrong idea of an IVF clinic, honey."

"Okay, so ..." Caroline looks at Amelie helplessly. "What's the deal here? Do we have to leave? There's a kid?" She's worried.

"Okay, okay, don't fret about that. The real deal is I might have a small surgery tonight to make sure they can use my sperm to get her pregnant." *Please let that be enough.*

"If that happens, I'll be sore for a few days and might have more appointments for a while. You should not be troubled." Amelie looks between the two of us.

"Wait, why would you need surgery? Don't you like each other? You kiss an awful lot for people who don't." Her eyes are bright and expectant.

"Sure, but things are more complicated." She has more energy after her nap than I've seen in a while. It's the depression lifting: even though something weird is going on—she has hope.

I have to do everything in my power not to shatter that optimism.

"Sorry to lie about the investment project. It was kind of private. But it's gonna pay for the rest of your surgery." I give her a reassuring smile.

Caroline frowns. "So we won't have to go away before the last surgery and my robot pants are ready?"

"Don't worry about that, sweetheart," Amelie speaks up. "If you and your daddy end up leaving, you'll be walking on your own two feet."

It's a big promise to make. But she's a fucking billionaire and she's Amelie. I've never met anyone as determined; she's so kind that sometimes I forget the strength underneath it.

I feel pathetically grateful when Caroline smiles and nods. "Okay," my daughter agrees. "But what about this other stuff?"

"Oh sweetheart, what's going on between your father and me shouldn't affect you." Amelie's voice is so warm and tender that for a moment, I think wistfully of the three of us as a family.

Then Amelie turns her gaze on me. "We'll sort out any other problems on our own." There's something in her eyes that makes me a little nervous.

Come clean about everything! She won't let any problems between us affect my daughter's care or housing—the only one getting a boot will be me. Except ... there's no goddamned way I'll talk about being a con artist in front of my daughter.

That's where I draw the line.

Putting it off for any reason is the coward's way, and I've been taking that route far too much. I excuse myself, thinking about that surgical table and the most uncomfortable ways this night could end. I owe it to Amelie, just like I owe her an explanation.

I'm going to let myself recover from those needles before facing the music.

Caroline has that dangerous little frown on her face again. I brace myself. "What is it, sweetheart?"

"How come you can't make a baby the normal way?"

Amelie nearly spits out her tea.

Oh God. "Your dad got hurt in the accident too and it might have caused some scarring that—"

Caroline's eyes fly wide open. "Oh no! You broke your—"

"I'm fine!" I interject, slightly panicked, never ever wanting her to finish that sentence. Ever. "It's just easier this way. You know, using a laboratory."

This right here is my fucking karma. I should have told the kid the truth somehow from the beginning.

I lie to everyone. I lied to Caroline about how bad she was hurt; I lied to myself about conning an innocent woman this intimately ... and I started out treating Amelie like another trophy.

I glance her way, and she's choking quietly into her napkin. This is probably awkward for her too, but now that Caroline's acting more secure, Amelie seems more amused than anything. Maybe hiding the truth from Caroline annoyed her?

Caroline nods, and then frowns. "So who's gonna be here if I have nightmares?"

"Edmund promised to stay all night, sweetheart. Chances are we'll be back in a few hours." Amelie pats my daughter's hand, and she smiles, reassured.

"Okay, good, I like him. He's nice." She returns to eating her breakfast.

Holy shit, that was awkward. But it went better than expected.

I wait to ask Amelie about it until we're in the car. "It was the right thing to do, but why insist I come clean with my daughter before we even hit the road?" I'm not trying for an argument, but she did seem awfully amused.

"When I was a little girl," she begins as we drive to the clinic near Old Jefferson, "My father lied to me all the time. He claimed to love me; he may even have done it to spare my feelings. But he lied. He lied when he cheated on my mother with call girls. He lied when he started bringing them home. He even lied when one of them stumbled into my bedroom, naked and drunk.

"He had a lie for everything and it never stopped. He even died while partying with one of his whores, without ever coming clean about anything."

Her voice is cold and bitter and I feel a stab of anger at that prick who treated his daughter that way. "I would never do something like that."

"No," she says in that same intense voice. "I don't know that. I only have your word. Do you love your daughter more than my dad loved me? Obviously. Are you better to her than my father was to me? Sure. But you can't claim to love people and then lie to them. And I don't want to have a baby with a man who is okay with that."

My heart sinks. "If you didn't have a point, I wouldn't have gone along with talking to her." My tone may be slightly grudging.

"You did." She sounds thoughtful. "Now just hold out for the IVF treatments, and you've kept up your end of the deal."

"Gladly." I feel relieved; absolved. Maybe I can get away without admitting my infertility was self-inflicted and part of a stupid plan.

Dr. Butler is a tall, statuesque blonde woman with a pursed mouth who looks me over, unimpressed, in her rimless glasses. She spends ten minutes explaining the technique. I'm to start, since my fertility test is the least invasive.

She hands Amelie a sample cup and the two of them share a glance before she looks back at me icily. "Deposit a semen sample and take it to my laboratory down the hall. If your sample is normal, we will test Ms. LaBelle's fertility instead."

"Whatever has to be done. I have a promise to keep." Amelie's face softens a bit.

"Very good. Try to hurry. If we need to perform a more invasive procedure, I'd like to get started promptly." Out of the room she goes, heels clicking briskly away down the hall.

I stare at the door and shake my head. "Yikes. She's a fertility expert but she could freeze a boner with a glance. This may take a minute."

Amelie moves toward me with the cup a gleam in her eye. "I'll help."

I open my mouth to make an awkward joke when she tugs the scarf from her neck and uncovers her cleavage. She unfastens the top couple buttons and her breasts swell further into view. "Holy shit," I breathe, my cock immediately at attention.

Bashful little Amelie has matured a lot in four months. And goddamn, here she is, making her first move.

"See, all you need is a little inspiration," she purrs, caressing my shaft with her slim fingers. I lean against the wall, chest heaving, and she cups the head of my cock in one hand.

I grunt and thrust against her; she teases and strokes me, nimble fingers circling the head and toying with the grooves and folds along and around it. Then she grips me more firmly and her hands start to pump up and down my length.

I relax immediately. *She still wants me.* Whatever Weiss said, he didn't ruin everything.

"Amelie," I pant, my balls tightening as she milks me. The slide of her hands over the head and shaft of my cock never lets up and I let myself go, groaning through my teeth.

I fight my instinct to last; her hand speeds over my shaft as I focus on the sensation and quickly start to shake. "It's coming," I whisper hoarsely, and she grabs the cup off the table next to her.

I pant harshly as my cock spurts my load into the cup, spattering the sides with cloudy liquid. Then the cover clicks sealed and I'm leaning, dazed, against the wall. "We good?" I mumble, astonished at how she can get me off even in a lab.

"For now," she says cryptically. "Let's see what the doctor says."

It takes me longer to catch my breath and push off the wall than it did for her to make me bust. I tuck myself back in my pants, zip up, and follow her, silk shirt sticking to my chest from sweating.

Amazing woman. Slightly scary. I have to win her for real.

The results are *almost* what I expected. "Although you are in good health and have the proper hormonal balance" the doctor begins as she leans away from her microscope, "you also have very few active sperm in your emission."

I try to react with disappointment as she mentions there were some sperm in my sample. Maybe this experimental gel stuff isn't so great, or perhaps Parikh didn't apply it correctly. No idea.

At least the presence of swimmers proves my tubes were not tied.

"This fertility stuff is complicated. How did our ancestors even get pregnant?" I sigh, hiding the mix of confusion and relief.

"Largely by accident," the doctor replies in a clipped voice. "We should do an ultrasound of your testicles to determine whether you can undergo a needle extraction with a local, or under sedation."

I freeze. The ultrasound could reveal the gel blockage. Again, the idea pops into my head: *just admit the truth.*

It will be embarrassing and make me look like an idiot and liar in front of both of them. It's better than having a chunk of one testicle removed—right?

Somehow, I can't say anything besides, "Okay."

Getting an ultrasound wand slathered in cold slime run all over my post-orgasmic boys is an experience I never want to repeat.

Amelie's with me the whole time, watching quietly. Am I more embarrassed or relieved that she's sticking loyally around? Once the ultrasound is over, the doctor whispers something to her and then turns to me.

"I'm sorry, Mr. Fontaine. The blockage is in the wrong place to allow for a needle extraction. We'll have to do the biopsy."

I look at her in slowly growing horror. "Oh." *Oh shit.*

My brain goes to war. On one side is *I didn't sign up to give up a bit of my bits* and on the other is *If I only had the gel removed months ago* and finally, responsibility wins.

"Would you have a razor and some lather I can use?" I joke gamely.

"The technician will shave you as part of preparations," the doctor replies in that same cold voice. "You will need to sign a few forms; one regarding the sedation, the others regarding the surgical procedure. Back in a minute."

She disappears into her office and shuts the door. I turn to Amelie with a wry look. "Well, damn."

"You sure about this?" she asks, her face unreadable.

"Look, let's put it this way. It's my fault you don't have a baby yet, and it's my responsibility to remedy that." And if I can avoid the super awkward conversation about *why* it's my fault, all the better.

"I'm glad you feel that way. But I'm still left wondering something. Why would Dr. Weiss hide the fact that you've got a problem from me?"

The breath freezes in my throat and I blink at her with glacial slowness, like a tortoise. "Uh, well ..." And I panic.

Staring down the barrel of something worse than a needle to my bits, I don't have the balls to answer honestly. I spit out "I don't know" almost reflexively and feel crappy and relieved when she frowns and drops the subject.

Phew, that was close. I'll tell her the whole truth someday ... after my balls heal. Maybe never, if I'm very, very lucky.

"I'm glad you're committed to this. It gives me hope." Another cryptic statement she doesn't qualify.

I hastily sign the papers, not even looking at them, wanting to get it all over with. The doctor whisks the papers away and sends me to the treatment room with Amelie.

The next ten minutes, my balls get shaved by a bored male nurse who bears an alarming resemblance to Homer Simpson. I avoid eye contact as a small part of me dies inside. *I am absolutely not telling my daughter about this.*

Finally, it's time for sedation. I'm draped on a surgical table, shaved, scrubbed, and feeling more vulnerable than a multiple black belt who is fucking a billionaire on the regular should. The anesthesiologist sets the line in my arm and monitors the machine as Amelie holds my hand.

It's sweet. It's what I do for Caroline.

She really does care about me. I'm one lucky sonofabitch. It's more than I deserve.

"I'll always keep my promises to you," I say drowsily, trying to ignore the scalpels and theatrically large-bore needles laid out on the tray next to me. The world's starting to get fuzzy. Soon I'll just have to tough through healing and it'll all be over with.

"That's sweet. It really does help," Amelie says rather coolly, catching my attention. "But you really have to work on telling the truth too."

My eyes can't open fully anymore; alarm slowly seeps through me, like cold water through a thick sock. "Huh?" I barely manage.

She leans over further as she whispers in my ear; I'm completely at her mercy in that moment.

"I know everything."

Oh ... shit ... is my last thought as I drift off.

16

AMELIE

A look of absolute horror on Daniel's face the moment before he falls unconscious is the most disappointing and satisfying thing I've seen in a long time. Once he's out, Emily comes in, chuckling, having dropped her icy demeanor. "So," she says, "What do you want to do now?"

"He doesn't need a biopsy, does he?"

She snorts and shakes her head. "No, your big stud is teeming with viable sperm; it just can't get past the blockages." She rolls her eyes. "He thinks fertility specialists don't collaborate. Once he started calling around, he became the local gossip."

"And Weiss?" How to deal with him? My lesson for Daniel is panning out well. I might even forgive him ... if he never repeats this again. But the doctor who he paid off?

What sort of punishment is good enough for that prick? Yet, if he hadn't gotten drunk and spilled the beans, I would never have suspected a thing.

"Weiss has taken an abrupt leave to parts unknown. He's running scared. Perhaps you should let him stir for a while." She checks Daniel's vitals and glances at his draped, nude form. "Hmm, I can see why you're thinking of keeping him."

I scoff and blush. "Emily."

She presses her lips and looks down. "I'll stop."

I lick my lips and look downward. "I should have come to you in the first place. I should have waited for you to come back from vacation. If I had waited just a little longer ..."

That's a slippery emotional slope: if only, if only. You can drive yourself crazy this way; break your own heart. I've been an expert in it my whole life.

"Thank you for helping me out," I tell my old sorority sister.

"The look on his face when he realized his con had blown up was more than worth it." She winks. "So ... now what?"

"I'm not doing anything he doesn't want." I keep looking at him. "He signed a permission form, but that's not the same as actual consent."

She removes her reading glasses, tucks them in her pocket, and shakes her hair out of its ridiculously severe bun. "According to my colleagues on the local mailing list, he's been looking to get the gel flushed out. Whether it was to get you pregnant or avoid fallout, that is not certain."

"I'm thinking both." I frown at him, weighing my options.

Half an hour later, Daniel's eyelids flutter and then slowly open. He looks at me, sitting beside him, and blinks sleepily. Looks like his memory is coming back as his eyes widen.

"Uh," he manages after a moment. "I ... still seem to have both my balls."

"Of course you do." I smile faintly. His comeuppance has taken the edge off my rage. "Lucky for you, I'm not a total bitch because I can afford it."

"Oh yeah, lucky. Very lucky indeed." He starts to sit up—and then winces. "What happened?"

"The doctor flushed your gel implants with bicarbonate solution, as you wished. According to her colleagues, you called most of them." My smile goes lopsided, watching his handsome face fall a bit more.

"I thought consultations were confidential," he grumbles, and I chuckle.

"They didn't use your name. It's a rare form of birth control here, and when she found it on the ultrasound, she knew who they were talking about."

"Wait." His eyes narrow, a mix of suspicion and astonishment. "Did you conspire with a doctor to manipulate me into thinking you were taking some kind of testicle-based revenge?"

I look him right in the eyes. "Did you conspire with a doctor to manipulate me into thinking you were fertile, while seducing me and playing head games for a bigger payoff?"

His mouth closes with a snap, and finally, in defeat, he nods. "Yes," he manages after a moment. "I did. Then I realized you did not deserve it and what a dick I was being—but it took me too long."

It's not a perfect apology, or the perfect truth ... but it's already a lot better. "Did you like it when I turned the tables on you?" I ask mildly, with my arms folded.

"Not one bit," he replies with a sheepish grin. "You really had me going for a minute there."

"Now you know a bit of what you put me through. And you have a chance to make it up to me."

My mother was never in a position, emotionally or otherwise, to hand my father real consequences for his actions. If she had, maybe she would have had a happier life ... even if he was too dim-witted to give up his bad habits. She could have at least had her pride ... and some sense of control over her life.

He swallows and nods. "If I proved I have what it takes." If he's mad at me for giving him a taste of his own medicine, he's not showing it.

"After all this? Yeah, that's why I'm not making your life harder." I step back as he slips off the table, the drape falling as he reaches for his pants on the chair next to mine. His freshly-shaved cock and balls look sleek and silky; I squash a flare of desire.

"I'm not sure what to do now," he admits as he gets dressed. "I thought you would toss me to the curb if you found out."

"Tossing you out means tossing Caroline, and she doesn't need that. I had to find another way to school your ass for lying." I help him into his shirt; he's still a little fuzzy from the drugs.

"I've certainly learned my lesson about lying to you," he chuckles, his eyes twinkling.

"Good," I reply. "Because if you ever try to swindle me again, I'm telling your daughter."

His mild look of dismay isn't quite masked by his amusement. He believes me. *He'd better.*

I guess I'm somewhat of a bitch, I think as we walk out shoulder to shoulder. *But a lady in my position has to be.*

17

AMELIE

Christmas has come again and for the first time in years, I'm not alone.

My hands are on my belly as I stand on the balcony, watching the storm clouds roll in, darkening the sky and giving Baton Rouge dusk at midday. It took months of trying the old-fashioned way before I conceived. But now, I'm looking forward to welcoming our first child by spring.

So are Daniel and Caroline.

It's funny how things work out. Dr. Weiss fled the country in a panic, so terrified of the consequences that he effectively exiled himself. If anything, he did worse to himself than I had even been contemplating.

That very night, Daniel and I tore apart the bedroom in a bout of make-up sex, ten minutes after making sure that Caroline was sleeping peacefully. I marked his back with my nails; he marked my skin with his mouth. We could not let go of each other.

In the first orgasm, I was squeezed between him and the wall, both legs locked around his pumping hips.

The second time, the third, on the floor with his face between my thighs, tongue darting mercilessly against my clit while his fingers explored me. The fourth, when he suckled it slow and soft instead, until I sobbed his name and lost my reason.

When we finally reached the bed, he pounded into me, panting desperately. I held him until finally, he pushed me down with his hips and felt the hot rush of his release. His soft moan sounded like music; he settled into my embrace and laid his head on my shoulder.

He spent that night in my bed and he's slept there every night since. It hasn't been perfect. But he's been lovely to be around—now that he knows where the line is drawn and what I won't put up with it.

"Out here, honey, you're gonna love this." Daniel's voice chirps over the faint whir-stamp of Caroline's early Christmas present as they get onto the balcony too.

I look at them, Daniel walking next to his daughter as she gingerly maneuvers her new exoskeleton out of the door. It's bulky, and the control cap will take some getting used to ... but she is definitely walking.

"These straps are itchy," she comments. Not a complaint. She's been feeling her legs more and more since healing from her last surgery and she points out every new sensation with fascination ... and optimism.

"We'll have them lined," I promise, and she smiles and nods as she moves to the railing. Daniel steps up between us and slips an arm around each of us.

I slide my hand into my purse and touch a button on a hidden remote. At once, millions of tiny lights blaze all over the garden. "Oh wow!" Caroline cries excitedly.

Daniel leans over and kisses my temple. "Not bad," he murmurs.

I smile and lean my head on his shoulder as the lights shimmer in the pre-storm dimness. Christmas has never been the common sort. We're getting thunderstorms instead of snow, Caroline got her present in a laboratory instead of under a tree, and my Christmas-Eve proposal came from a man that my father's family would never approve of.

My mother would, now that he's learned not to lie. And that's all that matters.

"Merry Christmas," I tell my new family tenderly.

The End

ABOUT THE AUTHOR

Mrs. Love writes about smart, sexy women and the hot alpha billionaires who love them. She has found her own happily ever after with her dream husband and adorable 6 and 2 year old kids. Currently, Michelle is hard at work on the next book in the series, and trying to stay off the Internet.

"Thank you for supporting an indie author. Anything you can do, whether it be writing a review, or even simply telling a fellow reader that you enjoyed this. Thanks

COPYRIGHT

CPSIA information can be obtained
at www.ICGtesting.com
Printed in the USA
BVHW041502030121
596862BV00006B/41